STUCK IN YOUR WORLD

Your World book 2

ANJ CAIRNS

Copper Rose Publishing

Copper Rose Publishing

ISBN: 978-1-9997944-1-5

Disclaimer

This is a work of fiction. Names, characters, places and incidents are either the products of the author's imagination or are used fictitiously, and any resemblance to actual persons, living or dead is entirely coincidental. Certain businesses and organisations are mentioned, but the stories playing out in them are wholly imaginary.

For Puffin and Nigel - the world is yours.

Chapter One

THE OVERPOWERING ARTIFICIAL scent of pungent tangerine and clove potpourri was the first thing he remembered about sixty-nine Stagshaw Drive, the first thing he remembered about anything. The second was the sight of a large, red-faced man wearing pyjamas styled as the kit of American football player. The man didn't have a ball or a helmet, but he burst through the door with the ferocity of an excited sportsman before stopping beside a bookcase full of CDs, videos and vinyl records. He bent over, gasping and wheezing, hands upon his knees.

"What...inhaler...asthma." The sound of erratic breathing combined with feet clomping down the stairs, along the wall-to-wall beige carpet and Aztec print borders and into the contemporary lounge furnished with a floral patterned three-piece suite.

"Oh my," said Clare Mackintosh in her M&S t-shirt nightie and pink foam noodles twisted throughout her flaming red hair. Her mouth stayed open, her eyes transfixed on the figure of a thin, dark-skinned teenager sitting cross-legged in the centre of her new Habitat rug, naked.

"In..hal..er," said her husband. She backed away into the hall of wall-to-wall beige carpet and Aztec borders and then returned with a blue plastic NHS issued life saver and handed it to her husband. He puffed once, twice and his breathing began to become routine, in and out at regular intervals.

"Steve, there's a naked man in our house."

Steve Mackintosh moved in front of his wife, his shoulders hunched, and fists raised.

"Don't make a move," he said to the undressed male sitting on the rug. "Clare, call the police. Nine, nine, nine, not the local number." The man on the rug moved his eyes between the two occupants of the house. They were a hazel brown colour and blinked every few seconds. The naked man said nothing.

"What do you think you are doing? You can't just break into someone's house and sit on their floor in your birthday suit. It's unhygienic." Steve stayed by the door frame, maintaining the distance between them in case nakedness was contagious.

"Well say something." Steve scratched his nose and spun his head towards the kitchen where a brand-new touch button phone hung on a pale-yellow wall. His wife was talking into the receiver to what he assumed was the police control centre.

"I've no idea if the lock is broken. Steve heard a noise. Yes, Steve is my husband, Steve Mackintosh. Me? I'm Mrs Steve Mackintosh. Clare."

Steve looked back at the naked man. Only his eyelashes were moving. Blink after blink with pupils dilated and eyeballs focused on a nearby piece of fluff on the floor which had escaped Clare's meticulous vacuuming regime.

"Don't speak then. We'll see what the police have to say. Thank God the government has taken a tough stance on crime. Probably bang you up for this. Breaking and entering, indecent exposure. Imagine if we had children? Imagine if one of them had walked in on you." Steve ranted, filling the silence with spontaneous, unfiltered thoughts.

"The police said not to go near him," said Clare reappearing behind his left ear. "They'll be here in about ten minutes. I'll put the heating on, shall I?" She shuffled off again in her sheepskin slippers.

Steve stood in vigil, moving from foot to foot, examining the intruder for clues of who he was or what he might be doing there. He guessed him to be in his late teens, maybe early twenties, younger than Steve himself but not by many years. A lack of clothing made ascertaining any more tough for the couple. His skin showed no visible acne, his face was clean shaven and the hue of his body, though dark, could have been Mediterranean or of pale Asian origin. Steve was rubbish at working out where people came from. More likely a care in the community case given the state of undress of their uninvited guest. He didn't look dangerous, sat with his modesty on show but Steve wasn't going to take any chances.

"Don't even think of trying anything. I'm allowed to protect my home, protect my wife against dangerous criminals. The law's on my side."

Clare stood in the kitchen, looking at their beautiful new gas cooker, the dishwasher, and fridge freezer adorned with a varied collection of magnets. How could something happen in a place like this? The marketing prior to purchase promised Greenlands would be safe, a place for families and people starting out on a journey through life together. A perfect location, a perfect home; no need to do the place up before moving in, everything a perfectly neutral magnolia canvas on which to apply your stamp at leisure. They had already begun the home transformation with the help of a growing pile of decorating magazines and multiple trips to the local DIY superstore. Never did she envision a starkers Buddha-like creature setting up camp in her lounge.

"I'm putting the kettle on Steve. The police will be wanting a cuppa at this time of night."

"A scotch would be better."

She sighed, pulling out a couple of tumblers given to them as wedding gifts.

"I'm not sure they will be able to drink on duty. And one of them will be driving," she said.

"It's for me love, not the police."

The doorbell rang emitting a neutral electronic ding-dong. Clare's parents brought her up knowing musical bell tones were common and she was determined there wouldn't be anything common about number sixty-nine.

"I'll get it," she shouted to Steve, making her way to the front door, which stood locked but not bolted. No need for added safety precautions in a lovely new residential area such as Greenlands.

"Mrs Mackintosh? You reported an intruder on the premises?" A couple of unruffled uniformed police officers stood on the doorstep holding up identification.

"Oh, thank goodness you're here." She lowered her voice to a loud fake whisper and cupped her hands around the sides of her mouth. "The thing is he's...he's got no clothes on."

"Thank you, Madam, we're aware of this. Whereabouts is the man in question?"

Clare pointed down the hall to the lounge where her husband and his ward remained in self-imposed imprisonment. The police officers paused to introduce themselves as PC Benjamin and PC Arnold before striding down the corridor, hands gripping their truncheons.

"Can I make you a cup of tea?" Clare's words trailed off. She shut the front door to keep the heat in and to stop the naked burglar becoming a streaker by making a run for it.

PCs Benjamin and Arnold scanned the lounge and exchanged nods. PC Arnold moved towards the man on the rug and crouched down.

"Hello Sir. Can you tell me your name?"

"He won't tell you sod all. Don't think he can speak," said Steve.

"Are you cold?"

Her colleague turned to Steve, whose face had puffed up with his huffing.

"Do you think you could get a blanket, Sir? So, we can cover him up."

Steve humphed.

"If you break into people's houses in the small hours and take all your clothes off, you can't complain if you're a bit chilly."

"I can't see any clothes Mr Mackintosh. Unless he's left them in the garden or by the back door. We'll have a look but in the meantime a blanket please Sir."

Steve went to speak then swallowed his words resulting in a hybrid noise, a cross between a gulp and groan.

With the room cleared PC Benjamin and PC Arnold continued to attempt communication with their suspect. Neither gentle coaxing or a sterner approach succeeded in soliciting a response, but the man's rapid, regular blinking stopped.

"Best call it in Arnold and request medical assistance. We're going to need a quack on this once." He turned to the naked man.

" We can't ID you, so you'll be John, John Doe, mind you there's a lot of them around, so I'll put you down as Michael; my son's called Michael." The constable jotted down the details in his regulation issue notebook.

Michael would remember snippets of this first encounter although the details would fade over the years until all that remained was a composite of mind pictures and fragments of phases. He would agonise over the smells, sounds, words of the night, interrogating them to find clues as to how he ended up there, as to who he was. For when Michael found himself in the middle of the Mackintosh's lounge competing for space with an ugly glass coffee table he didn't know where he was, who he was or what he was.

Chapter Two

TREVOR WAS A NEW MAN. He often felt like this, in most instances after meeting a new man, albeit for a brief dalliance. He wore the type of smile which caused people to imagine he might have been up to all sorts and in Trevor's case he usually had.

This time, he couldn't attribute his fresh view of life to some hook up or budding romance destined not to end in a fairy tale fashion. This time it was because of Sketch. Since December, the young woman (who had lived most of her recent life as one of the many energies working inside a computer to make it function in the way humans expect) had been staying with him. Having a new, younger flat mate who saw the world through the eyes of a child, with the awe and wonder they tried to teach in school religious education lessons, and with the day-to-day view of life as a beautiful adventure to be embraced, had transformed him. He'd not become a perfect specimen of humanity. He still growled with screwed up eyes until after his first cup of double shot coffee, failed to put the toilet seat down and never remembered to replace the empty cardboard loo roll holder with a roll he could use to wipe his bum. Sketch learned each of these things within days of moving in and altered her behaviour to compensate for it. Compromise was a key lesson learned by Sketch during her time in London, but she drew a bold double line under Trevor leaving his dirty pants in the kitchen sink.

"Pants live on your bum, or pants live in your chest of drawers or pants live in the washing machine or pants live in the washing basket. Pants do not live in the sink with unwashed pot noodle containers," she said, holding up a pair of designer boxer shorts with the tips of her yellow rubber gloves.

"They're clean," said Trevor shrugging his shoulders from his favourite spot on the sofa.

"But not going to stay like that as you pile dirty plates and cups on top of them."

"Ah well, they're just pants, I can buy new pants."

Sketch sighed.

"But you might not have a job soon. Don't you think it would be better to save up your underwear just in case? Saving's good, right?"

Trevor turned away from the TV, leant against the back of the sofa and looked at Sketch. Sometimes her logic could be damning.

"Ohhh, are you trying to burst my bubble? I'm trying not to think about the library. Let's talk about your hair instead."

Sketch moved herself in front of her reflection in a strategically positioned mirror. The mirror was good for the self-admiration she found humans enjoyed. It proved easy for her to fall into the habit of looking at her face, an avatar she'd selected before being sent to the human world, on a regular basis. Echoed back to her visual cortex was a young, olive skinned, oval shaped face with piercing green eyes. Her hair, platinum blonde, was styled with gel in to over-grown spikes.

"It's getting a little bit long," she said tapping the spikes gently with the soft pads of her fingers.

"Long? It's going to be classed as a deadly weapon if those peaks get any higher. Either that or men with ropes will start trying to climb them."

Sketch bent her head and lunged her way towards Trevor who ducked to the side sending her headlong into the grey sofa cushions. Sketch convulsed with laughter before spreading her guffaws like an infectious virus to Trevor, the pair them both in a painful cycle of uninhibited laughter. Sketch loved living with Trevor as much as he enjoyed sharing with her. She laughed, guffawed and giggled with him. *Everyone needs fun in their lives*, she thought.

"What you up to today then?" asked Trevor. Sketch looked down at her fingernails and bit her lip.

"Not much. Hanging out, the usual." Her voice drifted off as she spoke betraying her lack of nonchalance. Trevor sat up and manoeuvred her around, so they sat face to face.

"I think you should do something else, something other than keep trying to fix the computer. It's only making you sad and like my mum always said, the wind will change, and your face will get stuck like that."

Sketch screwed her face up and stuck her tongue out. She knew Trevor referred to the broken computer in the corner of the living room. The computer she had existed in as a trainee energy before being sent to London to learn what life is like for human IT users. While it remained a dead shell, she was stuck in this world with no hope of returning to her home in the Core.

"Come on, it's a little bit funny," said Trevor. "I'm just worried about you. Come in to the library this afternoon. Begw would love to see you."

"I suppose," said Sketch. "But, I can't stop wondering what happened to all the other energies. After a sudden termination engaging a proper transformation plan is complicated. And they might still be there. I might be able to save them." *Save them and go home*, she thought. It was one thing being in a different city or another country where the culture was alien to you but another to be in a remote world, in a form which was intended to be temporary. London and the people there had been kind to her. Being in the city had taught her much and helped develop a growing understanding of the human world, but she wished to be back where she belonged in the Core. If there was even the faintest chance of restoring power to the computer she had to keep trying.

"Babes, I get it, I do. Well, I kind of do. Some mornings, I think maybe I took too many drugs in my raving days because your life story sounds a bit trippy. But coming in and hanging out..." he raised his fingers in mock air speech marks, "with some crazy ass librarians might distract you for a few hours."

She flung her arms around her housemate and hugged him tight. Hugs were a definite advantage to living in a human form. Maybe she was fortunate not to have been transformed back to her world before the collapse occurred, but it didn't stop her thinking about those who remained, in particular Inco, her closest friend from the Core, whom she yearned for the most.

"I guess, I do love to be around you guys and all those books. There's something magical about books." She grinned, picturing in her head pages of novels, non-fiction manuals of how to dos, recipe books and histories. All which could be located online, in the binary code of the Internet, but there was something solid and permanent about print.

"Put some clothes on then," said Trevor grabbing his mobile phone from the coffee table. He looked around for his keys. "While I love your 'Star Wars kicks ass jim jams' you might attract some funny looks on the High Street."

She laughed and poked her tongue out in his direction before jumping up and ambling towards her small box bedroom on the other side of the London attic flat.

Chapter Three

MICHAEL SMITH AWOKE on Tuesday after weeks residing at the Finsbury Unit, the psychiatric ward detached from the main body of the 1950s hospital serving the new town of Hartington. It was the only part of the original Victorian estate of the Radley-Beauchamp family to have survived the German bombing during the Second World War. It retained a prettiness which came with age and a good gardener to cultivate the grounds. In recent years, the role of tending the outside space fell to a couple of volunteers from Friends of Hartington Hospital. They were encouraged to rope in residents from the unit to help with their recovery. Gardening was therapy and filled in some of the long hours of the day.

Inside, the building was characterised by vinyl flooring, faded carpets and walls painted a shade of green recommended to reduce anxiety. Such modifications resulted in a clash of old versus clinical and no nook or hideaway escaped the smell of medicated human beings and the pervasive stench of bleach.

At the end of the ward was Michael's bed, the last in a row of five. The bed allocated to Michael on arrival sat between those taken up by two older men, one with a diagnosis of schizophrenia, the other battling an eating disorder. Both were discharged within days, freeing up the window view for Michael. Rosy, the Ward Sister, arrived at the conclusion that although their silent patient still showed no signs of communicating with them neither did he appear to be a danger to himself. Medical investigations failed to find any physiological reason for his lack of language, verbal or non-verbal. There were no traces of drugs or alcohol in his system. All his tests came back clear and physically he appeared a perfect specimen for his age, which they estimated was between sixteen and nineteen. The police continued their enquiries into his mysterious naked appearance on the floor of the Mackintosh's living room and into his identity, but so far investigations failed to come up with any valid information. With no forced entry into the house, no one fitting Michael's description on the national missing persons database and a local media appeal resulting in fake claims, there was little left to go on. His file remained open but active police enquiries had been superseded by the need to track down a persistent flasher. Michael, no longer naked and entrusted to the care of the NHS, had fallen from the top of the priority list.

"You looking out that window again, Michael?" asked Sister Rosy during her rounds dispensing lunchtime medications. "Time for your pills. Mouth open. That's it, pop it under your tongue and swallow it down with a gulp of your water." He followed her instructions, not making eye contact or indicating he was aware of her presence other than his act of compliance.

"The night shift staff tell me you had another episode." She looked at his notes, registering squiggles about sudden awakening, his struggle for breath and the type of profuse sweating that required a change of sheets and an efficient bed bath. "No change though, good. Michael, I had an idea. Well, it was you that gave it to me." She manoeuvred around metal railings at the end of the hospital bed and perched on the mattress next to her patient. She looked him in the eye. He didn't look back. As a nurse in a psychiatric unit, she was accustomed to getting no response, but she sensed something in Michael biding its time, a pending reaction waiting for a catalyst. He was unlike any of the patients she'd worked with over the last twenty years nursing in the NHS. She understood her attachment to him was in danger of becoming more than was professionally called for, but a gut instinct moved her to allocate some time within the busy routines of the unit to encourage and nurture him.

"Since you spend so much time gazing out the window I thought a walk out in the garden might be an idea. That way you can breathe some fresh-ish air, smell the flowers, get some sun on you. Vitamin D is all very well in a pill but there's nothing like a bit of sunlight to top it up."

As expected, Michael said nothing. He remained seated in the same position, but Sister Rosy, unperturbed by his apparent lack of enthusiasm, happiness, disgust or dismay continued onwards with her plan. She pulled out some clothes, picked from the collection of garments abandoned by former patients, from the regulation cabinet beside his matching bed. Michael complied as she removed his pyjamas and replaced them with today's wardrobe selection, a pair of pale blue acid-washed jeans and a 'Frankie Says Relax' t-shirt, now too old to be deemed cool and not yet aged enough to have gained the kudos of retro clothing. She squeezed his head through the neck of a navy fisherman's jumper and flattened his thick, dark hair back into place. Once arms and legs were coordinated with the assorted items of mismatched clothes she stood back, smiled and nodded.

"That'll do you. Scrub up nicely, don't you? Let's head out then, it's quiet at the mo." She took him by the arm and led him past obstacles of beds and trolleys towards the door of the ward and outwards in the direction of the garden.

Michael processed life on the ward and the surrounding grounds as voices and colours, muted hues and tones, at times punctuated by loud, bright, gregarious bursts sent to assault his senses. Outside, lively arrays of spring daffodils, tulips and snow drops littered the fringes of the Finsbury Unit. He perched on a wooden bench next to the nurse who first brought him out here last week, fixated on the colours of the lawn, his nostrils breathing in the fresh scent of newly-mown grass after the first trim of the season. He absorbed the yellow of the daffodils, noting how they sparkled in the sunlight.

He rose, walked across the grass, treading down perky blades and knelt next to the spring flowers. He buried his face in their blooms, pulled them around his head, breathed in and exhaled with one word.

"Sketch."

Chapter Four

WINSTON OBILOGUI'S life had become a nightmare, a nightmare in which he found himself in the unenviable position of being forced to do what his employers paid him for; managing the Northgate cross borough library service. Recent events had resulted in a diversion from his masterplan to ride out his later years at the council by delegating a minimum of ninety-five percent of his daily tasks to his subordinates, including his long-suffering personal assistant Marilyn whose annual requests for pay increases above her pay grade he honoured, fearing she would resign if he refused. She was shrewd, and he knew the value of having someone to shield him from the barrage of emails, phone calls and video conferences which typified the average day at work for the average local authority civil servant. However, the hoo-ha which had arisen over the planned closure of libraries across the new metropolitan authority of Northgate exploded his comfortable routine and even Marilyn's effective management skills failed to prevent him standing smack in the centre of a media spotlight. One not unnoticed by his senior managers at the council.

It was clear to Winston who was responsible for putting a bomb up his established routine and he wouldn't allow them to get away with it. He double clicked on a desktop folder named BJ and perused the contents. Inside, file after file on the Kentish Town librarian Begw Jones detailed her recruitment, employment history and outlined the events leading up to her recent suspension, return to work and associated press cuttings. He garnered what he could from her social media profiles, but to his annoyance much of it was in Welsh and what was publicly available in a language he could understand was tepid and bland. Pictures of the Welsh countryside electronically painted with nostalgic filters and photos of lampposts sat alongside comments about tea and books and the importance of libraries. Nothing negative however, no dirt he could pin on her.

His inbox was angry, full of urgent-looking emails shouting at him.

"Do I need to read any of these?" he shouted through to Marilyn, at her desk on the other side of the glass partition. Her face remained composed as she arose, patted down her knee length skirt and sauntered into his office, two pencils holding her long hair in place like chopsticks in a bowl of noodles.

"Just the top ten, the least important are filtered out for you and I will deal with them in the next hour."

"Okay, I'll look at them in a bit. Pop out and get me one of those double shot, mocha strawberry supreme from Cafe Express if you have time. Use the petty cash. Don't look at me like that, drinks are an expense. I'm having a meeting."

"Err, there's nothing in the diary..." She flipped through her notepad.

"That's because it's a very small meeting. Just with me. Now off you go."

She sighed a sigh which he failed to notice. He never paid attention to anything she did as long as she kept the stress out of his work life. She could come in dressed as a comedy dinosaur and she doubted he would even register it. Still the job had its advantages, the pay was competitive, the hours sensible when compared with some of her graduate friends who worked in the city or for impressive-sounding law firms. Once she'd dispersed Winston's job load and fended off diary requests with the usual excuses such as what a busy man he was, she had plenty of time to do what she wanted to - writing a book, a book for children about living in a secret city underground away from adults, their rules and boring lives. Today, however, didn't look like a day for stretching the writing muscle, rather one where she be forced to humour Winston's fixation with the librarian Begw Jones by investigating those around her. First on the list to stalk online, a young woman called Sketch.

Chapter Five

CLARE MACKINTOSH ARRANGED to meet her mother on Tuesday. Although this was their regular day for coffee, shopping, talking about what was happening in the neighbourhood and the rise and fall of various characters on the television, the pair agreed to meet at the hospital garden. Mrs Wilson had long taken an interest in all things horticulture and prided herself on combining it with a hobby which gave something back, volunteering with the Friends of Hartington Hospital. There was little more wonderful than seeing something blossom from a tiny seed into a glorious flower, she had told her daughter on more than one occasion. Her years of weeding and seeding the historic grounds of Hartington Hospital's Finsbury Unit had earned her the badge of head volunteer and, after some cajoling, her pestering convinced the manager to allow her to be helped by residents. She continued to argue in favour of the therapeutic value of getting to grips with nature but believed it would all go to seed if she had to tend it all by herself.

Clare looked on as she approached the gardens. She smiled at the sight of her mother. At fifty-one, the older woman sported a full head of white hair, cut into a stylish blunt chin length bob. Unlike the generation preceding hers, Mrs Wilson frequented a pair of comfortable jeans and felt no inclination to settle for elasticated waisted trousers from Marks and Sparks. Clare's mum was a quite modern one, compared to those of some of her friends. Despite the welcome arrival of an early spring a chill lingered in the air. She wrapped her large cardigan around her and strolled over to where the work party was finishing up for the day.

"Hi mum." Mrs Wilson waved a pair of secateurs back in response.

"Darling Clare, there you are." She wiped some dirt on her overalls and squashed her offspring with a hug.

"Sorry, I'm late. Got stuck on the parkway. There's been a terrible accident."

"Has there? Nasty business. They keep building roads and making cars and wondering why people keep crashing into one another."

Clare stared at her mother.

"I know, I know. You should be used to the way I think by now."

"Oh I am." She squeezed her mother's arm. "Shall we get going? Do you want to change?"

"I should think so - not sure they will let me into Steve Lewis looking like this." Mrs Wilson laughed. "Hang on here. You might as well wait outside for me, given today is such a beautiful one."

Clare watched her mother disappear through the doors of the Unit and took some time to examine the spoils of a hard day's gardening. It was looking exquisite. At times, when visiting to pick up her mother, she would forget it was the playground of a building dedicated to mental health, that inside people struggled with severe depression, anxiety, delusions, those who found life in her world too much to cope with. The beauty of nature, of their surroundings seemed at odds with the ugliness of ill health. She shuddered. *There but for the grace of God* flitted across her thoughts and out the other side before she returned to thinking about what colour scheme to decorate the front bedroom.

"Sketch."

She halted on her way along the gravel path meandering around the outskirts of the building.

"Sorry?" Looking up from her mind wanderings she found herself staring at the face of Michael Smith.

"Oh," she said. She couldn't place him, his was face familiar, very familiar, but somehow out of sync with her memories. "Sorry, did I disturb you? Do you want me to fetch someone?"

The man didn't reply, but the memories came tumbling back as her hand found her mouth stopping them transforming into words.

"It's you." She looked around, realising she was alone with the naked man from her house, only he wasn't naked. Clare examined him, taking in his clothing, stance and the bag of garden rubbish in his hand.

"You talked. You didn't talk before. Oh, do you remember me? You were in my living room, before Christmas. You were..." her words trailed off. It didn't seem right to mention has lack of clothing now he was being treated for a mental illness. A looney, Steve had said until she shushed him, you didn't say things like that these days. While not the most politically correct of parents, her mother had grasped the changing language of mental health, because of contact with services and service users on a regular basis.

"What's your name?"

"This is Michael," said Sister Rosy who approached the pair from the side door of the ward. "Not one for chatting. Are you waiting for your mum?"

"Yes, we've met, Michael that is. He turned up in our house. I heard him talking just now."

"Did he say Sketch?"

"Yes, that's exactly what he said."

"Ah, that's normal. Sketch is your word, isn't it, Michael?" The nurse took Michael by the upper arm and nudged him in the direction of the main building. "Time for a tea break before you see the doctor."

Clare sank her hands into the pocket of her jeans, watching as the pair walked away. She had given little thought to what might have happened to the man after the initial search for his identity. After the break in, Steve secured the house with extra locks on the doors and used the incident as an icebreaker with the neighbours.

But then life carried on, work continued as did the battle against the multitude of magnolia painted walls throughout their new home. She pondered further. Was bumping into the intruder here, when meeting her mum, a coincidence? He appeared harmless, *but once someone appeared naked in your front room they held less of a threat*, she thought.

"You alright love?" said Mrs Wilson.

"Yeh, mum, I'm fine. Shall we make it a hot chocolate day?"

Chapter Six

"SKETCH," said Begw. "Trevor said you might be popping in. Got a job for you."

"Do you want me to cut your fringe?"

The librarian screwed up her nose, flicking loose strands of her chestnut brown hair to one side.

"I'm growing it out. That's what the clip's for. Isn't it obvious?"

"Errr, I suppose so. How long will it take?"

"Takes forever. Funny thing hair, especially Welsh hair."

"Really? Why is hair different on Welsh people?"

Begw sighed, air escaping from the side of her mouth and raised her eyebrows. The library was quiet. It not yet lunchtime, many of the regulars were still shopping or at the post office. Despite the widespread introduction of benefits and pension payments directly into bank accounts, most of the library's favourite readers still preferred to get their money over the counter at the post office's cash facility where they could have a chat with the assistants and the people popping in to send off parcels of belongings sold online.

"Let's grab a panad and I'll explain. Trevor's on the counter." Panad was the North Waleian word for a cuppa and although she ran an efficient library and expected a lot from her team, Begw was partial to a hot cup of tea or coffee and knew the value of building a conversation round it.

As the kettle boiled, Sketch flicked through magazines full of pictures of perfect people, advice to easily resolve problems and tips as to how to catch and keep a boyfriend or descale a kettle with natural ingredients.

"What's this job then?" asked Sketch. Her days had been harder to fill since her "return" to London. After her training period concluded, she had halted her transformation back to the Core of the computer. Sketch didn't leave the human realm, but her close friends, other than Trevor, believed she'd returned to her world. Her official return to London had helped halt the immediate closure of the library, but it remained at risk. Sketch's work experience place-ment had ended, leaving her at a loss as to how to fill her days, aside from struggling to fix the PC and restore the Core. A diet of daytime TV affected her view of the world. Her knowledge about the art and business of doing up and auctioning off rundown prop-erties for profit soared but she continued to be shaken by the people with problems who were encouraged to shout obscenities at each other on daytime television.

"It's the computers. Got problems, well on the blink and by rights the council's IT team should maintain them. But right now, I'm not in a position to ask for anything from Winston so..."

"So, you want me to help? I'm not so good with computers. Fixing them I mean."

"You're better at it than me. Give it a go."

Sketch looked around the library and spotted a couple of the older people from her beginners' IT class last year. As regular library members, the Silver Surfers group played a vital part in the ongoing campaign to save the local facility from closure. Mr Barrington waved at her, a smile spreading across his weathered face.

"Mr Barrington's been in asking to check his interbook. He's very upset he can't get on a computer," said Begw. Her face took on a *so what are you going to do about it?* look.

Sketch shrugged her shoulders and gave Begw a hug. The librarian stiffened.

"Does that mean you'll do it?

"How could I refuse Mr Barrington?" She grinned, the smile illuminating the expanse of her face.

"Hey, Mr Barrington, do you want to help me mend the PC?" she asked as he approached through a pathway of bookcases.

"Can I be your assistant?"

"Why of course."

After a little tinkering and a lot of joking with her second in command, Sketch ascertained the computers could be fixed without a major tech intervention. A couple of reboots and some deleting of programs which had somehow escaped the barbed wire of the council's IT firewall, and the machines were up and running again. Sketch gave Mr Barrington a high-five and helped him log on and link up with his online friends. She left him to type and went to pick up her bag from the staff room. Trevor sat on the faded green chair, decommissioning some old book stock for a sale at the weekend. He removed the barcodes from each book and stamped them as discontinued. There were less than usual. Under normal circumstances the annual library sale had tables full of novels, biographies and tomes of facts and historical retellings. This year, the offerings were slender as council officialdom had decreed a hold on new purchases until they resolved the matter of how they could close the library and use the money saved for other purposes. The campaign by local residents had resulted in a court injunction but Northgate council's legal team were putting in late nights in an attempt to overturn it.

"How are you doing, Sketch?"

"Super good," she grinned at Trevor and twirled around in front of him. "The computers are fixed. If I can fix some here I might be able to fix Jackie's too, don't you think?"

"Of course, you can. You are the superstar of fixing things and you know that computer inside out, literally inside out."

"Have you seen my bag?"

"Here you go." Trevor pulled a khaki backpack from underneath his chair. "Your phone's been ringing by the way. It was Jackie. I had a peek, didn't think you would mind." He faked a sheepish expression and then laughed.

"What did she want?"

"I didn't answer it. Even I wouldn't answer your calls, but she did send you a text saying you should go around and see her. Said it was urgent."

Sketch walloped Trevor on the arm.

"Trevor, why didn't you tell me?"

Chapter Seven

WHEN CLARE BEGAN to visit Michael she did so covertly, under the guise of helping her mum with the hospital gardening. Her cover was in part to avoid awkward questions from Mrs Wilson but also because she couldn't find the right words to tell her husband she was spending time with a man in a psychiatric unit, the same man who had appeared naked in their living room in the darkest hours of the night. She had tried, but her attempts to broach the topic met with a bullish response.

"I wonder what happened to the man," she said, setting down a cup of instant coffee on the side table next to her husband's reclining armchair. Slouched in it with the TV remote control at his side, he looked to her every bit the married man. Dependability had been one of the things she once adored about him, at the time when she said yes to his proposal of marriage. His safe, respectable job for a well-known insurance company, the deposit for a mortgage and enough income so she would only have to work part-time, allowing her to enjoy their new home had sounded like a perfect proposal. Over the weeks and months of cohabiting in the morally acceptable manner of man and wife it began to dawn on her that "enjoying the house' was Steve-speak for keeping it clean and pristine, looking every bit the show home they saw when viewing the development of the estate to choose a plot. But not working more than three mornings a week at the bank as a teller left her sufficient free time to take up gardening with her mum.

Steve glanced up from his copy of the 'Daily Mail'.

"What? Oh coffee, thanks, you're a love."

"I was saying, what do you think happened to the man from the living room?"

"The looney? He's where he belongs, in the looney bin with the rest of the nutters and schizos. The police told us. Can't say I give two hoots as long as he doesn't come sniffing round here again. This is my castle."

Clare cleared her throat but swallowed back some of her words, the ones telling him it was politically incorrect to say looney bin or schizo. He was a man of cemented opinions, so she chose not to waste her breath.

"*Your* castle?"

"Our castle then. As long as he doesn't pop up again during the night."

"How can he? We've had all the locks changed, fitted an alarm. It's like Fort Knox in here."

"Once again my beautiful wife you are right. How about we go out to dinner tonight?"

Clare smiled at him, rearranging her menu plan for Saturday in her mind. The chops were already defrosted but she could cook them up in a casserole for one of the days next week when both of them were working.

"Pizza?" asked Steve, returning to a story about how immigrants were stealing jobs from people like him who owned castles.

Clare joined her mum at the unit every Wednesday morning. Therapeutic horticulture worked better before lunch as the stodge of a carbohydrate rich but bland meal mingled with various cocktail of medications to numb the responsiveness of the patients. Many of the patients were long-term residents of the unit and initiatives became more a means of timetabling their daytime hours than a meaningful attempt at rehabilitation. By April 1991, Sister Rosy thought of Michael as in the 'unlikely to ever live in the community' category. His diagnosis of a dissociative fugue state was now being questioned by the psychiatric team, but he continued to be uncommunicative. He followed simple instructions but stared into nothing looking like he couldn't focus his eyes to see people and things in front of him. His body language gave nothing away; his posture neutral and his blank facial features unwavering. In keeping with this, Michael remained silent, expect for a regular repetition of the word 'sketch'. No one understood what it meant to him although it became a game amongst the care team to guess.

"He might be an artist or an art teacher."

"Or it could be his name."

"Sketch? No one is called Sketch.

"Could be a second name or short for something."

Despite the guessing, nothing changed in Michael's behaviour and his treatment regime settled as it became apparent that medications either numbed his senses or pushed him further into his waking coma; they had no effect.

Michael learned much during four months of being looked after like a child. He took in language, dress and fashion, patterns of behaviour, tone of voice, social expressions and status. He collected them like coins in a piggy bank, guarding this treasure for a future time when he would begin to employ them. He discovered he was a man, not fully grown, not physically mature or mentally complete. His living coma allowed him to grow into this strange, gangly body with its unrelenting growth of hair on his head, face, legs, arms, pubic area and under arms. He observed that all humans had some degree of hair on their bodies, but he couldn't fathom the functional nature of it. Michael memorised hair, it became the primary way he recognised people in his life. It was how he remembered Clare: the woman with ginger undulating strands, falling below her ears but stopping short of her shoulders. Her hair brightened on days when the sun chose to shine on it as she weeded in the garden, days which were few and far between but transformed the rust of her strands of hair into copper wires, weaving a multitude of coils around her square shaped head. Today, clouds blanketed the sky, but he still recognised her as he walked from the overheated building to the gardening party across the lawn. She waved at him and moved her lips into what he now knew to be a smile. As he approached, she rose from her knees and handed him a solid plastic gardening fork.

"Hi Michael. How you doing today? Thought we would do a bit of weeding this morning. Doesn't matter how often we clear this area the blighters keep trying to take over."

He felt something in her presence but didn't yet have the words to describe it. She guided him over to a patch of earth populated by both flowers and weeds.

"Look out for the little blue ones, they look pretty but they're infamous for strangling their non-weedy neighbours." He breathed in and out, processed her words and kneeled down.

"Dig down with the fork and then give them a hard yank. That will make sure we pull them up from the roots."

He followed her words and began creating a pile of discarded undomesticated plants from root to flower.

They worked in a companionable silence as Michael took in the sounds of their movements and contrasted them with bird song and the low-pitched rumble of traffic from nearby roads.

You're doing an excellent job there," said Clare. "Half wish you could come and help out with our garden. Steve's not interested and there's so much to do." She paused her digging and pulling, rubbing at an itch on her nose with the back of her arm.

"Our garden's not anything like this, mind. The house is a new property, well you know that don't you? You've been there. Did you see the garden? Expect not, it was dark that night. Steve's more interested in having barbecues in the summer than planting things and I think he's forgotten we live in Hartington." She laughed.

The cloud cover grew murkier as they worked and before the scheduled end of the session drops of rain began to plop onto the ground.

"Oh," said Clare. "Looks like it's going to tip it down. We best get you back inside." She gathered up their forks and kneeling pads and placed the pile of unwanted foliage into a wheelbarrow rusting at its corners.

"I'll see you next week. Off you go back in before it gets any heavier." She waved as he walked back towards the main building. "Bye Michael."

"Bye."

Chapter Eight

THE FRONT DOOR of the Townsend's home swung open as Sketch, with Trevor in tow, launched herself into Jackie's house. Although she no longer lived there, Jackie insisted Sketch keep hold of a set of keys for emergencies, so she always had somewhere safe she could return to.

"What do you think she's going to say? Do you think it's about the Core?" asked Sketch, fidgeting with the sleeves of her top.

"Dunno. It could be anything, but we'll find out soon enough."

"Sketch? Is that you?" Jackie's voice filtered up from the basement kitchen, her head emerging from the bottom of the stairs as Sketch and Trevor made their way down.

"Hi, Jackie. Yes, I'm here."

"And so am I," said Trevor from behind her.

"Hello Sketch. Hi Trevor, I didn't know you were coming."

"Oh," said Sketch. "It's alright that he's here isn't it?"

"No, Trevor you must leave now," said Jackie, her face serious. Sketch looked between them, swallowing down chunks of air and scrabbling around in her brain for appropriate words.

Jackie and Trevor laughed. The older woman rubbed Sketch's back.

"I'm just joking, hon. Of course, it's alright for Trevor to stay. He's always welcome here. In fact, you might be able to help, Trevor."

"Me? I don't know anything about computers."

Jackie beckoned them into the large, homely kitchen dining room, gesturing to the centre piece wooden table.

"It's not about the computer. Have a seat, I'll make us a cuppa and explain."

A combination of relief, sadness and panic assaulted Sketch. Her heart pumped faster than usual, and she felt unexpected tears appear in the corners of her eyes. She pulled a tissue out from the pocket of her skinny black jeans and dabbed them away. Trevor was preoccupied with an unsolved Rubik's cube lifted from a box of games sat on the table.

"I've not seen one of these for years. Used to be a cube genius."

"I found it in the loft," said Jackie as she squeezed the life out of some supermarket own-brand tea bags. "Lots of retro stuff up there. Old consoles, redundant cables, the works. Even some floppy discs - now they're no good to anyone."

She returned through the arch dividing the basement into kitchen and living space with hot drinks for them all and a packet of malted milk biscuits; they were one of Sketch's favourites.

Sketch made a grab for the biscuits and hugged her cup of tea under her chin.

"So, what's going on? If it's not the computer. Is everyone alright? Ashling, Matt, Sammy?"

"Don't worry, they're all fine. They're out at the zoo today with Dominic. A treat from Matt's dad."

Like most families, the Townsend's situation could be described as complicated. Following her divorce, Jackie had lived alone in the Tufnell Park house with her teenage son Matt. This changed with Sketch's arrival from the Core and the revelation that Matt was the father of Ashling's young son, Sammy. Thanks to an accidental intervention by Sketch, Ashling and Sammy now lived with the Townsends. The extra support allowed Ashling to return to college part-time to finish her studies.

"What's it all about then, Jackie?" asked Trevor.

"This morning, I had a visit from the authorities. It was about you, Sketch."

"About me? But I haven't done anything." Sketch bolted up on her chair, leaned across the table towards Jackie. "Have I? Have I done something wrong?" The room seemed darker to her, like when something happened in the Core, like the mistakes she made which resulted in her being sent here to the human realm, the world outside the computer.

"No, well, it's not your fault. The thing is someone has reported that you're under eighteen and you should either be at school, college or on some sort of training like an apprenticeship."

"Who would have done something like that?" said Trevor. "How do they know how old she is? She's not..."

"Human?" said Sketch. "It's okay, to say it. I'm not human, not one of you. I don't want to be. I want to return to the Core, to be a computer energy like I used to."

Jackie moved around the table, so she was sat side-by-side with the young woman. She took Sketch's hand in her own.

"We know that, and we love you for who you are but until we find a way to return you we've got to make sure you're safe." She turned to Trevor.

"In answer to your question, we had to give information when Sketch was doing her work placement in the library. A couple of years ago, this wouldn't have happened. But they changed the law and now not being at school or training 'til you are eighteen is a criminal offence."

Sketch bit her lip.

"Will I go to prison?"

"No, honestly, don't worry about it. No one will be taking you anywhere. I'm recorded on all the paperwork as your guardian, so I'm responsible."

"Will you go to prison?" said Sketch, horrified that her existence might result in negative consequences for her human friends.

"I'm not going anywhere but we don't want too many questions asked about you. We don't have answers to them and I can't see a social worker believing you come from a magical realm inside a computer. The paperwork doesn't have a tick box for magical realms." Jackie gave a half smile and patted Sketch's hand.

"So, what do we do?" asked Trevor.

"Something practical." Jackie rose from the table and picked up a glossy A4 pamphlet from the top of a pile of papers languishing on a little dusted piano. "Begw says it's impossible to give you another work placement, what with the dispute of the library."

Trevor umphed, puffing air out of his nose as his face appropriated a frown.

"But there are other options. What about doing a college course?"

"Me?" said Sketch, her eyes alive with the embryo of an idea.

"Yes, you."

"But what would I study?" she asked.

"Doh, that's obvious," said Trevor taking a chomp on a malted milk. "You do an IT course or an apprenticeship - it'll help you fix the computer. It's a win win."

Chapter Nine

SISTER ROSY ARRIVED at the unit with a cake and a packet of balloons. It was her birthday, but the party wasn't planned for her. It was a goodbye for one of their long-term residents, Michael Smith. Neither the consultant psychiatrist nor the care team were reassured he was ready for independent living but his remarkable progress over the summer coupled with budget cuts and a trialling of the new care in the community initiative catapulted the decision to reintegrate him into the world beyond the hospital. Since his breakthrough moment with Clare in the garden, Michael's language and communication skills had grown at an unprecedented rate. His progress was comparable to a child who doesn't talk then begins to speak with full sentences rather with tentative fragments of words and phrases. The cake, a lemon drizzle from the food section at Marks and Spencer, was a small way of celebrating his achievements.

In the preceding days, a pervasive chill had crept into the air, but the team felt it fitting to hold the small party outside in garden. The guests included Mrs Wilson and her daughter Clare, who continued to visit Michael although a change in her working hours meant she could no longer volunteer with the Friends of the Hartington Hospital. A couple of trestle tables were laden with plastic cups, cake, crisps, hummus and carrot sticks, and a good luck banner of shiny silver foil was sellotaped to the front.

Michael Smith examined his belongings. His worldly goods amounted to a tiny proportion of the things you would expect to have accumulated by your late teens. The pile on the bed made up of hand-me-down clothing, some well-thumbed books and out of date magazines, toiletries and notebooks he used to move his thoughts from his mind to words and pictures captured on paper. He still couldn't remember anything before his naked birth in suburbia, but medical opinion placed him biologically between the ages of sixteen and nineteen years. The courts designated a provisional date of birth document which would allow him to participate in the world, gain a driving licence, a passport and open bank accounts, all the necessary gateway documents for living independently as a citizen in the UK. The lawyers at the hospital accelerated the process, arguing that he couldn't take part in the care in the community trial without them and alongside pressure from their local MP this meant everything was in place for Michael's departure. Should he regain his memories, changes would be applied but for now Michael Smith was eighteen years, two months and three days old.

"Michael, hi," said Clare detaching her arm from her mother's to hug him. He liked hugs. "Your big day then?"

"Yes, today I leave." He looked down at his feet. "I'm scared."

"Of course you are, it's only natural to be a bit nervous. The move is a momentous change, but you'll be fine. Won't he, mum?"

"You'll be more than fine, especially with this one keeping an eye on you," said Mrs Wilson. "Shall we get some cake?"

He nodded and laughed as Clare rolled her eyes.

"You and your cake, mum." They piled up with snacky party food and found a space to sit on some of the plastic school type chairs borrowed for the occasion from the group therapy room.

"Michael? Are the flashes still happening?" asked Clare.

"Ummmfs," he said, through a mouth full of salt and vinegar mashed up potato chips.

"I think that translates as yes," said Mrs Wilson. Michael's flashes of light and darkness occurred at random, freezing him like a statue and, though he didn't understand them, the pulsating flashes didn't scare him. Medical investigations failed to find a cause for them, ruling out epilepsy and other brain related abnormalities. Much like his memory loss, his condition remained inexplicable making him a medical anomaly and of great interest to the doctors not just at the Hartington but around the world. Papers were being written about him. Michael Smith was a case study darling.

"Can I have everyone's attention please? Drag yourselves away from the refreshments for a minute or two." Sister Rosy stood up.

"Today, and I think I speak for everyone here, we are proud, and a little bit sad to be saying goodbye to Michael Smith." She turned to face Michael and smiled the smile where he could see her eyes twinkle, one of the human signs of warmth and love. He smiled back, his cheeks lighting up with twinkle.

"Michael, you've achieved so much, and we'll be here to support you as an outpatient, but you're ready to take on the world now." Michael was conscious of all the eyes looking not at Sister Rosy but at him. He opened his mouth but couldn't speak.

Sister Rosy pulled a gift-wrapped box from behind her.

"We've had a whip round, and this is just a small gift from us all, something to remember us by - that's if you even want to remember us." A twitter of laughter did the rounds as he took the present from her, touching the shiny paper, turning it upside down and exploring it with his hands. He lifted it to his nose and sniffed, causing the assembled group to laugh further.

"Open it then," said one of the nurses. He peeled away the Sellotape careful not to rip the paper and unfolded the wrapping. Inside he found a wooden box engraved with the words, *Michael's Gardening Tools*. He undid the metal latch and discovered a trowel, a fork, some gardening gloves, packets of flower and herb seeds and accompanying blank labels.

"The gift is so you can carry on your gardening. Even if it's just in pots or with a little window box," said Mrs Wilson. "I hope you like it." Michael felt the urge to cry, happy tears they called them. In therapy, they encouraged crying, with happy tears being the best kind.

"I'm...I'm..." he said, choking on the words.

"Not speechless I hope," said one of the psychiatrists. They chuckled, and each began the rounds of wishing him good luck and giving him assurances that their support would still be there after his departure.

Interrupting the goodbyes, Clare tapped him on the shoulder.

"Sorry to interrupt but I've got to go. Steve's expecting me back, so we can go to dinner with some of his work colleagues. It'll be another evening of me glazing over at the talk of insurance and house prices," she half-laughed. "I'll give you a ring tomorrow at the Lodge and see you on Friday. Don't worry, remember there are plenty of people to help you make this work."

Chapter Ten

ALTHOUGH LATE IN the year for students at the local college to be starting courses, Sketch made an appointment to discuss her options including whether she could be accepted onto an apprenticeship scheme; learning as she worked and gaining some qualifications at the same time. Pieces of paper asserting you were able to do something proficiently trumped real-life experience in the human world. Sketch realised taking out time from her own attempts to breathe life back into the redundant PC meant delaying a potential return to the life she was supposed to be living. However, she argued with herself it also increased the chances of her success. A little voice in the hidden regions of her brain whispered that learning would also give her a backup and career options should she not be able to return to the Core. She didn't like the voice and tried to squash it by singing catchy boyband charting hits whenever it attempted to speak to her.

Jackie's house was on the way to Northgate Centre of Education and Training or 'the college' as it was known as to locals. Ashling and Matt were both attending classes that morning, with Sammy in the subsidised day-care paid for by Jackie and her ex-husband.

Sketch arranged to walk with them, so she called for them on the way.

"Sammy, hold on to Sketch's hand," said Ashling, walking alongside them with her bag over one shoulder and her hands pushing his buggy. "He won't make it all the way, but he loves to walk."

Sketch held tight to Sammy who wriggled and pulled at her hand.

"Yef. Brummmmmmmmmm."

"Hang on speedy, we're coming in a minute. Are you going to school with me?" The little boy nodded.

"He's being a car now," said Matt. "Some days I wish he pretended be one of them eco buses."

"Environmentally friendly?" said Sketch.

"No," said Matt. "Silent."

"You take no notice of daddy, he's just tired," said Ashling. The college was a twenty-five minute walk with Matt's school only fifteen. He kissed Sammy and said goodbye to the other two.

"Good luck with registration, Sketch. Soon you'll be doing homework every night too but at least you won't have to get up and change nappies or stop a teeny tiny crying thing," said Matt.

"You love it," she said. "Bye." He sloped off leaving them to continue on to the college.

"Is Matt okay, Ashling?"

Ashling swerved to avoid a magazine distributor as he waved a free publication in front of them.

"Careful, Sammy. Yeh, he's fine. Like I said, he's tired and worried about coursework and exams and stuff."

"You've got all that too."

"But I'm used to it, well not the homework and studying, but after being at home on my own with Sammy for all that time I love being able to use my brain. For Matt, it's the other way around. He's given up uni and parties..."

"And girls, he's given up girls, hasn't he? I don't think he's had a girlfriend since Britney," said Sketch. They paused at the roadside waiting for the electronic men to turn from red to green.

"Do you think he might want to marry you?" asked Sketch.

Ashling stared at her, mouth open.

"What? No! I don't think that at all and I certainly don't want to marry him. We're fine as we are, and he knows I'm with Dominic. Me and Dom are tight."

The lights changed and they crossed, joining the tide of young people climbing the steps to the college entrance.

Ashling, Sketch and Sammy went their separate ways. Sketch was sent by a monotone, bored looking receptionist to the second floor, through a corridor of student art and design projects to room 2.8. Never having been part of formal learning before, the data download provided to her when she transformed from a computer energy to a human gave her the bulk of what she needed to know for day-to-day life. However, much of her most valuable learning came from residing with a family, working and living as a human and experiencing emotions such as loss, unrequited love, pride and happiness. The complexity of human life still amazed her, and she was keen to be able to apply this knowledge to her duties as a computer energy. The technical side of how a PC functioned from a human perspective was unknown to her. No one in the Core had expected her to be stranded indefinitely in a world where she didn't belong. The option to learn more, to be part of a student body and to have a student card to go to the cinema at a discounted rate, lightened her.

She knocked on the door, the kind of knock impossible not to hear, and waited. Not receiving an answer, she peered through the small lined glass window in the door. Inside sat an imposing gentleman, whose body appeared to be oozing out through the gaps on his chair. The headphones clamped on his ears explained his lack of response. She pushed through the door, walked over to the end of the computer bench where he sat, stood beside him and watched as he typed code onto the keyboard. She doubted he knew that each of his keystrokes was respond to by a computer energy, trained to respond to his commands.

As he reached the end of a sequence he raised his fingers from the keyboard, flexed and clenched his fingers and rolled back his shoulders.

"Oh, who are you?" he asked, sitting up on his chair and angling his eyes in her direction.

"Sketch, Sketch Smith. I'm here for an appointment to talk to Atif about apprenticeships." She held up her phone, showing an automated confirmation text.

"Really? They didn't tell me about it." He speed-typed a login to the NCET staff network and pulled up his calendar.

"Oh, here you are. Sorry 'bout that. Means I'm not prepared but since you're here let's have a chat. I'm Atif by the way." He swizzled around in his chair and indicated for her to sit on a matching one opposite.

"So how can I help you? Apprenticeship is it? Off the top of my head, we've got spaces in administration, I'm always being asked for admins and catering. Spot came up last week with one of them celebrity chef programmes. You any good at cooking?"

Sketch steadied herself, put on her best smile, confident but without cocky body language, and addressed Atif eye-to-eye.

"Actually, Mr err, Mr."

"Atif, Atif will do."

"Thanks, actually Atif I want to do an IT apprenticeship. I want to learn how to fix them. Last year, I helped old people learn how to use them, but they keep breaking, the computers not the old people, and if I could fix them I'll be able to put everything right."

Atif picked up a felt-tipped pen and chewed it at the wrong end. Blue ink coloured segments of his lips and an odd squiggle appeared on his chin as he spat out the pen.

"My advice for you, Skid," he began.

"It's Sketch."

"My advice Sketch, is don't eat pens. They don't taste good and are possibly poisonous."

"Okay, but what about the apprenticeship?"

He shrugged. "Don't think we've got anything fits that at the moment. Let me have a think. In the meantime, we can find you some paperwork to complete. Make sure all your details are on the forms and I'll get back to you."

"How long might it take?"

"The paperwork? At your end ten minutes, at our end weeks and that's being optimistic. The wheels of low level bureaucracy turn slower than a slow thing."

Sketch slumped back in her chair. This was an unexpected outcome, and one which didn't help solve either of her problems. Jackie still might be prosecuted if she couldn't prove Sketch was engaged in training and learning, and without new skills the solution to unlocking the Core remained out of her reach.

"Is there nothing you can do?" she asked. "I'm really keen and I learn quickly."

"Look, this is a bit unorthodox, but my little brain has had an idea. Got to run it past someone so give me your email address and I'll be in touch."

Chapter Eleven

THE LODGE WAS A SMALL, purpose-built residence for people leaving long-term residential care, historically as a prisoner and now as someone making the transition from mental health wards to the community. Generic furniture softened the clinical nature of the rooms. Architects designed the building to make attempts at self-harm or taking your own life that bit less possible. Residents were encouraged to add personal touches to communal areas and their rooms in the shape of photos, ornaments, un-killable house plants such as spider plants and cacti. A couple of cushions and a matching throw given to Michael by Clare as a moving in gift and a pot of basil, which he'd grown from scratch with the seeds in his gardening box, adorned his room. Bright green leaves sprung from regular watering and the occasional chat to the edible plant, and at mealtimes Michael selected the biggest of the bunch, adding them to his plate regardless of the type of food he or his housemates were serving up. The plant lived in his room, under his care, he didn't want anyone jeopardising its lifespan by taking too much or over watering its soil.

His room was small, the size of a student room in a traditional style hall of residence at a university. In it lived a single bed, a chest of drawers, a compact built-in wardrobe and a wooden desk and chair. Its minimal space didn't concern him. He loved it because it belonged to him, not forever but for now. Other residents, of whom there were five, had to ask permission to enter and if he left a sock or pair of pants on the floor no one complained about the mess or asked him to pick them up. Despite this freedom, his room was spotless. The Unit at Hartington Hospital had stamped onto him a sense of order and cleanliness. The same couldn't be said for all his flatmates. The communal areas, bathroom, lounge and kitchen were never as clean or tidy as he liked. He found plates left in the sink to grow a skin of food which needed soaking or determined scraping to remove, shoes were abandoned by chairs, and bags and coats were often found littering the floor. Rather than annoy Michael, the chaotic nature of his fellow residents intrigued him, and his curiosity expressed himself with questions which attracted strange looks.

"Rebecca, how do you feel when you don't clean the bath?" he said to his next-door but one neighbour.

"Feel like? Don't feel like anything. I just put the plate down and gets on. Next, you'll be asking me what the bath feels like. It's a bit like therapy this."

Rebecca joined Michael at the Lodge a week after he moved in. Both new, they hung out together, watching TV, going to collect their benefits from the post office and picking up the bits of shopping needed to keep themselves fed and watered. She liked to talk a lot, Michael liked to listen and ask questions.

"How long were you in for?"

"This time, nearly three years. The folks couldn't cope so signed me up with the help of our family doctor. Three years of this medication and that pill and every therapy you can think of from group to art. I once created a sculpture of my boobs out of matchsticks. It gave the shrinks something to talk about," she laughed.

"You must have been a kid when you went into hospital?"

"Ah, you're sweet. I'm older than I look. Twenty going on sixteen. Still get asked for ID in pubs and clubs."

Michael also delved into Rebecca's relationship with her family, producing more questions than answers. They had the means and space in their house, but they lacked the capacity to take her back into their lives. Instead, they attempted to compensate for their lack of personal support with money and gifts of music systems, albums, TV and clothes. From Rebecca's answers Michael surmised that the expensive presents didn't compensate for the lack of visits or her parents' reluctance to let her return to home.

Music blared from Rebecca's bedroom, guiding Michael towards it. He noted the tune was music to dance to which was confirmed by Rebecca as he reached the source of the noise. She danced, raved, waving her hands in the air, oblivious to Michael's appearance; lost in the rhythms of the sounds emitting from her CD player.

"I'm mad for it. Are you mad for it, Mikey?" she said as she spun around to face him. He watched from the doorway. He knew how much Rebecca loved the music, and as she continued to pirouette, jump and oscillate he thought she appeared the embodiment of life, what it should be when at its best. Free from thoughts and worries and not wondering who you are and where you came from and why you don't feel right in your head or at home in your body. With her straight, mousy brown hair that fell to her shoulders and her hyper-active behaviour, Rebecca differed from Clare. Clare was solid, safe, married with a job. Everything she achieved in her life made her seem, to him, to represent adulthood. She was so sure about herself compared to Rebecca who didn't seem certain about anything. She said she was, but Michael watched her, noting that her actions were reactive and random. She threw herself into everything like she was running down a road blindfolded and ignoring any of the possible cars, people, obstacles she might hit along the away. He thought perhaps that ignoring the things she didn't like was how Rebecca got up in the morning.

"Michael, there's a ginger bird here for you," Dave yelled up the stairs, the sound of his voice battling with the bass of the music. "Shall I send her up?" Michael looked again at Rebecca swirling around to the beat of a club CD. She looked beautiful.

"I'll come down." He pulled his gaze away from her spiralling limbs and the curves of her body, resetting his attention to his guest.

The Lodge's lounge was functional with a seating area for six, although it was unusual for everyone to be down there at the same time. Clare perched on the cushion of an orange sofa, noticing how the quality differed to the expensive one purchased by her and her husband from a well-known department store when moving into their house.

"Clare, this is a surprise, a pleasant surprise," said Michael. "Sorry, I didn't hear the door. Rebecca's got her music on." Clare nodded. She tensed at the mention of Rebecca and Michael wondered why. They had only met once before, and it seemed wrong to him to judge someone on a single meeting. He couldn't recall anything which would cause dislike or other uncomfortable feelings.

"Mum wanted me to invite you round for dinner on Saturday," Clare said.

"That's thoughtful of her. I've never been invited to dinner before," Michael added it to his mental list of firsts. He rubbed his head. "But I can't come."

"Really? Steve won't be there if you're worried about that. He's off on a stag weekend. Used to be people had a night out before their wedding, now they have a weekend. Please come, it would mean the world to mum. She's not seen you since you moved in here."

"Sorry, I can't. Rebecca asked me to go out with her and I said yes."

"Oh." Clare swallowed. Michael sought the appropriate words to stop her being disappointed. Any other time he would love to take part in a family meal, but Rebecca had asked first.

"Another time maybe then," she said.

"Yes, okay. Please say thanks to your mum from me. Will you explain?"

"Yes, of course. So where are you going with Rebecca?"

"Just to the cinema." He looked away as he spoke hoping she wouldn't know he was lying. They planned to go clubbing and he sensed Clare wouldn't approve.

"I'll see you on Sunday at football anyway, you can still come?"

"Of course," said Michael. "Looking forward to it."

Chapter Twelve

WINSTON OBILOGUI LIKED to make an entrance. He enjoyed the power surge that accompanied a crowd of eyes trailing him as he walked towards the service desk at Northgate Central South Library. He ignored the unspoken code of the library, quiet at all times, blundering his way past children and adult service users. He banged his fist on the buzzer at the customer counter.

"Hello, hello, is there anyone there?"

Begw popped out from behind a bookcase, pushing a trolley half-full of returns to be re-shelved.

"Oh, it's you, Winston. we weren't expecting you. There was no memo."

He frowned at her, eyes narrowing. A local library manager shouldn't cause anyone this much hassle and why did she insist on calling emails memos? Did she think it was the 1980s?

"It should be evident to you that as Head of Library Services I don't need to make an appointment."

He stared at her, willing her to blink or move first. If this was a shootout at high noon he'd be the one coming out of it alive.

Begw rolled the trolley out of the path of the public, moved behind the counter and put her hands on her hips.

"What can I do for you, Winston?"

"It's come to my attention that last year you employed a minor without my knowledge or approval."

"We've not employed anyone since we laid off Gita two years ago when you instigated another round of cutbacks." She used her fingers to make virtual quotation marks around the final two words.

"What about that girl, Sketch?"

"Firstly, Sketch is a young woman not a girl, secondly, she was not employed she was on a work placement and thirdly, I have paperwork in the office with your signature on showing you okayed it."

A rage blew up in him, the sort of anger which made him want to shout and throw things around, but he wasn't in his office and this wasn't his PA Marilyn. He'd survived all these years by knowing when to shout and when to store up his anger for later.

"Maybe close your mouth Winston or, as my mam used to say, the flies will get in." She reclaimed her trolley of novels and non-fiction tomes and strode off to finish her book shelving.

Winston turned to leave and saw Trevor laughing from behind a carousel of paperback romance novels.

"You can laugh, you'll be laughing all the way to the Job Centre soon."

Jackie checked her email. The laptop her ex-husband had lent them so Matt and Ashling had something to do their homework on performed every task faster than their older cumbersome computer, but to Jackie it lacked character and history. She knew, because Sketch had told her enough times, that energies lived inside all computers, responding to the commands of their human users. She understood there wasn't just one Core but millions of them all with energies waiting in the background to be booted up and leap into action. A couple of years ago, the One recruited her as a liaison between worlds and while all of the science was explained to her at the time, she couldn't recall the details of how it all worked. But for the existence of Sketch and experiencing her phase in and out of their family living room, she would have talked her doubting self into believing her mind made it up during a psychotic breakdown, or a flashback from cocktails of drugs taken in her younger clubbing days.

She frowned at the screen, refusing to acknowledge the energies within while mail appeared one by one in her inbox. The messages were on the whole unwanted newsletters she kept meaning to unsubscribe to. She scrolled through them, deleting those with subject matter pertaining to cheap flights she still couldn't afford and chose not to take because of her careful watch over her carbon footprint, local meetings she didn't have time to attend and random campaign petitions she knew she should sign but would never get around to. Her eyes alighted on an unexpected email from Begw. She clicked and scanned her eyes across the content.

"Crap." Begw's email alerted her to Winston's visit and his accusations about Sketch's work placement. Following so soon after the intervention from the social worker, her guess was Winston had reported them to the authorities.

"Sketch," she said, her voice raised to a level that would reach up to Ashling and Sammy's bedroom on the ground floor. Sketch lumbered down the stairs, a packet of Jaffa Cakes and a half-drunk cup of earl grey tea in her hands.

"Jackie, you should see what Sammy just built with the bricks. He's a genius architect in the making."

"Imagine that. He doesn't get his building skills from me, all I could ever make was a flat roofed house with some basic windows and doors." Jackie patted the empty sofa cushion next to her. Sketch sidled up next to her, enjoying the warmth other human bodies emitted.

"How are you getting on with the college application?"

"Still waiting. The man in charge of apprenticeships has a friend in the college who he's talking to about making an apprenticeship for me there, in the IT department. The idea is I can learn on the job and help them with their maintenance."

"How long do you think it will take then? A few days, a week?"

Sketch shrugged.

"Could be tomorrow, could be next month. Why? Has the social worker been back?"

"No, but it would be good to have something sorted out before we meet with her on the tenth."

"Don't worry Jackie, it'll be alright."

Jackie laughed. Sketch sounded just like her talking to the youngsters in the house.

Chapter Thirteen

REBECCA HAD ARRANGED to meet up with her friends before heading over to Paradise. That was as much of the plan Michael knew. She rifled through the meagre contents of his wardrobe, rejecting items as unsuitable, drab or things that made you look like someone's dad. He wondered whose dad she referred to.

"Those jeans, I mean no one, no one wears those anymore."

Michael shrugged, they were all he had, a pair of jeans, a pair of jogging bottoms and pair of chino knock-offs a care worker had donated thinking they might be useful for job interviews - so far there'd been no job interviews.

"Just as well you're about the same size as me, skinny boy. You can borrow one of my t-shirts." She bobbed off to her room returning with a bright yellow tie-dye oversized top.

"Put this on." She stood watching as Michael stripped off his green polo shirt and put on the replacement.

"Look at you, your new look is perfecto," she looked him up and down, smiled sideways at him and kissed him on the cheek.

"Tonight is going to be fabulous."

Andy, Rebecca's friend from her time at school before being hospitalised, lived close to the centre of town, a bus ride away from their accommodation. The area was comprised of rundown rented accommodation, bedsits and houses crammed full of more people than they were designed for. Graffiti clung to brick work and dustbins, weeds crawled from gaps between paving stones and unraked gravel on front gardens, and empty cans of super strength lager littered the verge of the road. Michael took in everything under the orange glow of council street lighting. His heart rate accelerated, and goose pimples arose on his arms; Rebecca had insisted he leave his coat behind. Despite the unfamiliar environment, Michael was comfortable with the darkness. Bright colours may be beautiful in nature, but his borrowed tee shirt dazzled him, made him queasy. There was something simple and uncluttered about the dark.

The interior of the Andy's small flat reflected the exterior of the building, unkempt and smelling of stale sweat, unwashed dishes, sheets and human male. On a battered sofa sat two men sporting long hair and middle partings, long-sleeved tops rivalling those in Joseph's technicoloured dream coat for most colourful garment in the world award, baggy jeans and trainers.

"Alright?" said the chunky, tall man, rolling tobacco into a cigarette paper. Rebecca nodded.

"Alright. This is Mikey," she said pushing him towards the sofa. "He's the one I told you about, my "care in the community" mate." Her fingers air quoted care in the community. "He's a guinea pig, like me."

"Mikey, is it? Welcome Mikey, I'm Andy, this is Julian but he's as wet as a girl, so we call him Julie. Want a fag?"

"Err no," said Michael. "Hi, hi."

"Best off, filthy habit but I loves 'em. Nothing like having a ciggie, especially after a bit of nookie." Rebecca and Julie laughed. Michael nodded and laughed too although he didn't know what nookie was. He made a mental note to look it up in the dictionary.

"Bit quiet in here," said Rebecca. "Bang some tunes on."

"Help yourself," said Andy. He took a drag on his cigarette, held the smoke in his mouth and exhaled, creating nothing more than a large smelly cloud. "Crap, thought I'd cracked the smoke ring."

Rebecca rummaged through a crate of cassettes, some in plastic cases and others thrown into the pile. She held up a tape.

"Where did you get this? It's really rare. I mean, a Firemaster mix on tape, didn't even know they existed."

"It's who you know, Becs. There's this geezer, posh bloke, bit like you but still living with his olds." Michael noticed Rebecca wince. "His dad works with this guy whose son spins tunes in clubs, does Ibiza in the summer. Swapped this for some gear."

Michael struggled to keep up with the conversation as it took a turn into words and phrases he didn't understand the meaning of; they were speaking an untaught language. He stayed quiet, storing everything away to process later. When he left the unit, Michael realised there was a lot for him to experience but didn't comprehend the extent to which the world would be complicated. His psychiatrist tried to prepare him for this and they continued to speak at length about newness and how to cope in unfamiliar situations. Their appointments had decreased from once a week to monthly and while the community care mental health nurse team provided back up and occasional in situ support he felt disconnected, an orphan of the state. Rebecca understood. Clare tried to understand but her life was too different, too normal. A cavernous gap of understanding sat between them, and besides her husband didn't like her seeing him. Rebecca shared with him an understanding of what it was like to be out of sync with the world you live in. Right now, however, she fitted perfectly with the small group, leaving Michael as the odd one out.

She pressed play on the plastic stereo system, turning the volume to the highest point on the dial and filling the room with vibrations of base and the hypnotic sounds of synthetic drums. He closed his eyes letting himself blend into the rhythm.

"Michael...Michael."

His eyes snapped open. In front of him three sets of eyes stared in his direction.

"Dude, now is not the time to sleep, now is the time to party," said Julie.

"I'm not asleep, I was..." said Michael.

"You were what? Meditating like a hippy? 'Fess up - you was

getting some shut eye Mikey, innit?" said Andy. "Out of it, totally out of it. Look when we hit the club, you're going to need something to keep you going. It just so happens I got just the thing." Andy took a small-sized match box from the pocket of his jeans and popped the drawer open. Inside sat a clear plastic bag containing round white pills. "Is he alright to have these?" Rebecca nodded.

"Meds don't work but this will. Take one," she said, handing Michael a can of half-drunk lager. "Swig it back with this. You're gonna be amazed how you feel. Take it now and it'll be kicking in when we get there."

"What is it?" he asked.

"A pill, E, Ecstasy. Where you been living mate?" said Andy. Rebecca stared at him, her face frowning. "Oh yeh, sorry. No offence. Take it, it's a freebie, and tonight is going be tops."

The effects of the pill came on before they reached Paradise. He became talkative, no longer scared to share with Andy and Julie. It didn't matter if they used strange words because they liked him, even it was only because of his friendship with Rebecca. His insides were warm, glowed. Sweat dripped from his forehead as he danced but he enjoyed the sensation, it enriched him.

THE LIGHTS PULSATED, strobing, flashing, changing from colour to colour, working through a rainbow-like spectrum. Michael's body vibrated with them, with the music, the most perfect music for the most extraordinary night. The lights, the sounds, the bodies all moved together. He could see with clarity now, he was supposed to be part of this, this here, Paradise, an oasis without palm trees or nature but the beauty of the humanity, moving together as one. All the time in the hospital, at the unit, in the garden and later in his new home was worth it for this single night. He belonged. At last he was part of something spectacular. He leapt in the air to the tribal beat of the current track, arms pumping, waving, exploring the space around him.

'I love you," he shouted to Rebecca. "I love everyone." She twirled, pulled his face across to hers and kissed him. He pulled away and grinned. "I love kissing." He touched his lips lightly on her eyelids, over her face creating brief, soft points of pressure.

"Woooo," said Rebecca. "Life is love." She hugged him, squeezing up close and then danced off in the throng of sweat and euphoria. The love remained as he danced, grinning at the beauty of humanity. Why had he not seen it before? Not realised how the music can free you?

Track blended into track. Michael paused to glug back some water given to him by a girl he danced next to. He need the toilet and weaved his way through the jostling bodies with outfits blazing colours to his eyes towards the illuminated loo sign at the corner of the bar.

"Michael, mate," said Andy. "This is the balls, innit?"

"It's everything. The world is beautiful. Where's Rebecca?"

"Over in the corner, snogging the face off this night's love."

"Rebecca's beautiful, that's why everyone loves her," said Michael. Everyone loved everyone else, that was okay, he saw that now.

"Sure, everyone loves our Becs. Be careful mate, you can do better than her," said Andy. Michael frowned, scanned Andy's face and then laughed.

"You're so funny. You're my best friend, except for Rebecca." He threw his arms around Andy, who patted his back.

"Whatever, mate, whatever."

Chapter Fourteen

SPRING TERM WAS COMING to an end and the college would be closed to students for two weeks. Lessons and tutorials stopped, and homework was assigned in the form of essays and reports to be handed in after the Easter holidays. Jackie's concern over her not being in either education or training worried Sketch. She wanted to get it sorted out, so they could go back to focusing on restoring the Core. The more time passed, the less chance there was of returning to her world and she yearned for the company of her own kind. In particular, she felt the absence of Inco. Always the sensible one, always the successful one, always there for her; but back then she didn't appreciate the importance of his attentions, not until all the energies disappeared for what might be forever. In circumstances such as this she knew he would advise her to take action, not the jump-into-a-pool-of-sharks-with-your-eyes-closed type of action but the sort which gives you a chance of making a change. With the visit from the social worker imminent, she decided to go back to the college and attempt to tackle the matter before the holidays began.

Atif had stopped replying to her daily emails but she tracked him down to the college cafeteria by questioning random students she met in the main building.

"Atif, it's me, Sketch." She sidled onto a bench opposite him at the end of a long row of trestle tables. He looked up at her, then back down at the laptop and exhaled a sigh as he shut the lid of the machine.

"Sketch, what can I do for you?"

"I brought you a latte," she grinned at him and pushed the paper coffee cup across the table. "I like to buy people sausages but sometimes they're vegetarians and they don't like them as much." Atif opened the lid of the coffee and peered at the contents.

"It's a double vanilla banana pie latte with extra cream," she said. "Everyone likes those."

"Thanks Sketch. Happens I'm quite partial to hot sugar and cream. Does the sudden arrival of coffee mean you want to talk to me about the apprenticeship?"

Sketch nodded. "Yes, it's super important or Jackie's going to go to prison." Her grin disappeared from her face. "I mean, she could get into a lot of trouble and who knows what will happen to me."

Atif rubbed his eyes.

"I have tried to push it but my mate, and it's not that he's not keen, but he's been having a few problems."

"So, if he takes me on I can help him. His problems disappear, my problems disappear, social workers disappear."

"I wish it was that simple. Give it a month."

Sketch sank down further down onto the table wishing there was a double vanilla banana pie latte with extra cream in front of her, because the meeting wasn't panning out the way she'd hoped it would.

"Hey, look I know it's not what you want to do but there's this new gardening short course starting up. It's got spaces, if you enjoy it you can go on to an apprenticeship at a local garden centre, or you can transfer and pick up the IT stuff once Mick's back."

"Sounds okay," said Sketch. "I don't know anything about gardening, but flowers are lovely, and food is tasty and I'm excellent at eating it."

"Gardening it is then. In addition to the practical weeding and seeding you have to complete basic English and Maths tests but you get credit for them, and they'll count towards your apprenticeship NVQs should you decide to take that route. Hang on while I fill out this referral form. You'll need your guardian's consent and the usual info, name, address, qualifications. Do you have any qualifications?"

Sketch shook her head. "It was not being qualified that got me into this pickle, but I super absorb information, so it won't be long before I get some. It's so exciting." A vibrancy returned to her eyes, her fingers and face fidgeted, and her mouth joined in the smiling.

"I can't wait to tell Jackie, oh and Trevor, he's going to love this."

"All done," said Atif, gathering up his pile of papers and laptop and taking a large swig of coffee. "Let's pick up this form from the printer and get you to registration. Then you can leave me alone for a couple of weeks, right?"

Sketch punched him on the side of his arm.

"Joker," she said taking his arm as they dodged bags and jackets trailing from benches. She knew the coffee would make something happen.

"Here you go, just sign here, below my signature and put today's date." He handed Sketch a college issue pen.

"Nice," she said. "Can I keep it? As a reminder of how you saved my life?"

Atif chuckled. "It's all yours. Now take the form home and bring it back with your guardian's signature and they'll give you all the course bumf. Starts on Tuesday morning, I believe."

Sketch spun around as a comfortable warmth crept through her veins. A course, a free pen and a qualification. It was the best day in weeks.

Chapter Fifteen

IT TOOK Michael a little short of an hour to walk the two miles from his hostel to the town park where he planned to meet Clare. Steve's nephew played in the local five-a-side league for under tens and despite her dislike for the sport she had agreed to spend Sunday morning watching competitive parents shout at the referee. Michael wondered again if it was a good idea for him to join them. Steve didn't seem like the type of man to hang around with a former naked intruder, but Clare had told him not to worry. She thought it would be educational for him to see something of normal life, get some fresh air and share a cone of chips and drink coffees from the park cafe.

His anxiety about seeing Steve again fed into the thickness in his head, the black sense that nothing would ever be good again, nothing would be as amazing as last night. At Paradise he felt alive, part of something incredible, beautiful, a place where he slotted into the confusing jigsaw of life. Now he was just a weirdo again, a thin, brown, tired strange being without a clue to who he was or why he was. The sun squeezed out from behind dark clouds making him squint. He wrapped his jacket around himself and watched the world laugh at him as he trudged down a tree-lined avenue of houses where people lived with their happy families: sharing break-fasts, watching TV, laughing, planning holidays. Knowing they belonged.

The park typified green spaces built into new towns to give people areas to play or get together with their neighbours. Divided into zones, the football pitches were at the far end, adjacent to a small building housing changing rooms which smelt of mud, sweat and dirty football gear. In contrast, the path Michael took to reach it was scented by flowers, grass trimmed to a uniform height and edged in straight lines. He stopped to take it in. Whatever mood took him, nature settled him. It was bigger than him and his feelings. The natural world existed regardless of the intense despondency and murk he couldn't shift.

At the end of the previous night, the group had reconvened at Andy's flat, added to in numbers by a man Rebecca had made friends with on the frenzy of the dancefloor. The music changed pace to a mellow, quieter vibe, and Andy encouraged Michael to share a spliff, claiming it would smooth the transition as he came down from his pill. He refused it. It had a noxious odour, worse than cigarette smoke and he didn't like the way smoke clung to his clothes. As he walked through the park, he wondered if perhaps taking the drugs was a mistake. The after effects of the E were more than unpleasant. He continued to shuffle through the park contemplating whether to turn around and go back to bed. Rebecca was still in bed when he left.

"Michael, Michael." He turned his head. Clare waved at him. She stood next to an overflowing rubbish bin outside the cafe. "Over here."

He attempted a smile, but it didn't sit well with his face, like the smiles left behind in the brilliance of the previous night.

"Hi Clare."

"What's up with you? You look like you've lost a pound and found a penny."

He snorted air through his nose. "Pardon?"

"It's an expression. Just means you look a bit fed up."

"Suppose I am."

"Was the film rubbish? That can throw your mood. Let's grab some coffee or maybe even a sneaky hot chocolate. See if we can't cheer you up."

She led him into the cafe, holding the door open as he slouched through it. "Go and sit over there, I'll pay for these."

He took off his jacket and found a table by the window, the floor to ceiling glass offering a view of the children's play area. He rested his chin in his hands and observed Clare as she bought the drinks from the counter. On most days, he enjoyed her cheeriness, her advice and support, but today he wished it away. In his head he pictured her side-by-side with Rebecca, Clare the older one with a job and a husband and a house and a balanced view of the world. Rebecca in contrast was his age, had wonky brain wiring, was unemployed and lived in a half-way world. Both were attractive, but Rebecca pulled him towards her with an invisible string, winding him in tighter and tighter. Clare's hair was the prettier.

A cup of household brand hot chocolate appeared in front of him, its smell seeking out his nostrils and providing a brief moment of distraction from his thoughts.

"Here you go," said Clare. She pulled up the chair opposite. "Some days are like this Michael, it's okay to be down now and again."

"Suppose." His eyes flitted from the hot drink to the play area and across to the counter.

"Tell you what, you're lucky you missed dinner last night. Mum burnt the main course and then the cat decided to have a go at the pudding before we had a chance to tuck in. You should have seen mum's face. She bought it all from Marks and Spencer's too, must have cost a small fortune."

Michael looked at her. She was expecting him to say something but everything he ran through in his head sounded stupid, or miserable.

"Lucky for the cat," he said. Clare laughed. He had said something stupid, should have kept quiet when his mood was so dark.

"Sorry Michael, I'm laughing cos the cat's called Lucky. You couldn't have known that."

"Oh. Listen Clare, I'm not feeling well. Do you mind if I go home?"

"No, of course not? What's wrong? Is it serious?"

He shook his head. "I think might have picked up a virus."

"In which case you should go home, take a paracetamol and tuck yourself up under the duvet. Get some sleep. Do you want us to give you a lift? The match will be over in twenty minutes."

"Thanks, but I'd rather walk, be outside in the fresh air for a while."

"Ok, but I'll call in after work tomorrow and check on you."

Chapter Sixteen

THE LOCAL COMMUNITY centre was five minutes' walk from the library, off a main road but in a popular residential part of the area. It too was at risk of closure because of cuts in funding. The land on which it stood would bring in colossal amounts of cash for the council if they were free to sell it. The building had become a hub for local protests about everything from fly tipping to the lack of time spent by privately contracted carers on each of their clients. It was also home to the campaign to keep the library open.

Mr Moore, the appointed head of the recently formed Friends of Northgate South Central South Library was putting out a circle of chairs when Sketch, Matt and Trevor arrived.

"Let us give you a hand with that," said Matt. "How many are we expecting tonight?"

"Had ten people say they're coming on the Facebook and Mr Barrington dropped a note in my door saying he would come after watching the local news."

"Neil the lawyer?" asked Sketch.

"He's sent his apologies. Busy at the office. But he's sent a report to Begw and myself." He scrolled through some documents on his iPad and passed the device to her. "There's no good news I'm afraid."

Chairs filled up, with local residents of all ages whose passion for the library had helped halt its closure at the end of last year. Since then there'd been a lot of online campaigning but a hiatus of action from the council as Neil the lawyer provided pro-bono advice and legal letters to get disciplinary action against Begw lifted and prove the council had not consulted with local residents about the planned closure.

"Evening everyone," said Mr Moore. The few conversations going on dropped to a murmur. "Thanks all for coming out. The agenda includes the usual things about online posts and keeping our profile high with the local press but we've one big item to discuss. Begw, do you want to explain?"

The librarian rose from her chair, being short she liked to stand when talking to a group.

"Thanks Mr Moore. The management have sent me a proposal and asked for it to be read out, so they can gather people's views on it. This is part of their official consultation."

"Does that mean they have to listen to what we say?" said Annabel Bradford, who as the official secretary for the group jotted down minutes of the meeting to a spiral-bound reporter notebook.

"It's a consultation, so they have to ask people things but, in my experience, they rarely care what you say. It's a tick box exercise."

"So, we make them listen," said Mr Barrington. "We did it before."

"This time's different."

"Why?" asked Sketch.

"I reviewed the wording on the online surveys and feedback forms. The questions are biased but in a subtle way, and they have plans to put them everywhere, so no one can accuse them of not talking to a big enough number of people. Neil says them doing it will be enough to shift the legal judgement," said Begw.

Mrs Harding-Edgar put down her knitting and snorted.

"We won't stand for it. You're talking like it's all over and we all know it's never over 'til the fat lady sings. "

"We're not giving up," said Mr Moore. "There's plenty of opportunity for us to get people to fill in this here consultation."

"Yes, we can give them pointers on what would be helpful to say and keep up the messages about why the library's vital to the local community," said Begw. Around the circle, heads nodded in agreement.

Chapter Seventeen

ON RETURNING TO THE LODGE, Michael went straight to his room. One challenging conversation was enough for today and he thought if he lay on his bed and closed his eyes he may be able to recreate the sensations of the night before. He pulled his curtains closed, stripped down to his boxer shorts and t-shirt and slipped under his duvet. His bedding, washed earlier in the week, retained the artificial yet comforting scent of summer breeze. What would he tell his psychiatrist about the weekend? On one hand, the doctor had encouraged Michael to experience new things, move outside his comfort zone, but on the other hand Michael imagined the psychiatrist would frown upon him taking an illegal drug. Perhaps he could share about the clubbing but not the drugs; half-truth through omission.

He wrapped himself up, cocooning his body from the outside world. The last time he had slept was Friday night and with eyes closed and thoughts spiralling he moved into the zone between waking consciousness and the escape of sleep.

A thudding on his door brought him back into the day as he jumped awake and looked around.

"What? Where am I?" The room appeared familiar, but the

terror pushed his heart to beat faster and adrenaline to course through his veins. He listed the things around him, a tactic suggested by the mental health team in the unit for incidents such as this. Bed, duvet, green curtains, magnolia walls, alarm clock, notebook, desk, chair, herbs growing on the window sill. The banging continued.

"Michael, Michael, can I come in?"

He breathed out. It was Rebecca, Rebecca was his friend and they lived in a hostel because both of them had been in hospital. Rebecca was beautiful. He scrambled into his jeans, shook out his duvet and sat on top of the bed, legs crossed.

"Yes, of course."

Rebecca's face appeared around the door. It looked like a disconnected head, he thought, a head smiling at him, skin smooth and hair swept up in a ponytail.

"Hi, how are you doing?" she said.

"Two out of ten. Not brilliant. You?"

Rebecca fiddled with her ponytail as she moved into the room.

"Rubbish, I hate this bit, comedowns suck. Can I come and sit with you? I don't want to be alone right now."

Michael's brain struggled to process this because a big part of him wanted to be alone in the dark with his thoughts. He wiped the sweat from his hands down the side of his jeans.

"Yeh, join me. Not much company I'm afraid. Not like last night."

Rebecca positioned herself next to him on the bed and leant her head on his shoulder. "Did you have fun?"

He turned to face her, trying not to create any more distance between them despite her closeness making him nervous.

"I did. Rebecca, it was incredible. How can something so tiny make you feel so good?"

She smiled into his t-shirt.

"The music, the people, the love," she said. "It's worth the crap mood afterwards to have all that. It frees me from life. Life can be a drag don't you think? The rules, so many rules."

Michael leant over and tapped her on the nose. She laughed.

"Get off my nose."

"Sorry," he said moving his hands away from her.

"I'm joking. It was nice, in a Michael way." She lifted her head and looked at his. They were inches apart and her breath landed lightly on his face.

"Was it?"

"Yes, it was. You're nice."

"Oh."

"I'm glad you're here. No one else is here for me."

"What about your parents? Andy and Julie?"

She bit her upper lip and Michael saw the colour of the soft red skin darken.

"My folks don't care. They think they can throw money at me and their duty is done, and Andy and Julie, well they're alright but they haven't been where we've been."

"I'm sorry. I won't leave you, I promise," he said. Stray strands of blonde hair fell across her cheek. His hand shifted upwards, drawing it behind her double pierced ear. He attempted to slow his breath in the way the therapists taught him.

"You won't?"

"I won't...I..."

He froze. What next? What came next? His thoughts were halted as Rebecca's lips met his and his physical responses took control. He was being kissed, kissing a beautiful girl. First there was E and then there was a kiss.

Chapter Eighteen

MONDAY MORNING HAD A BAD REPUTATION, thought Clare. Instead of being back to work and drudgery, it was the day she got the most done. She worked a half day starting at twelve-thirty and used the hours before to get set up for the week, make lunches, pick up bits from the shop and make sure all the ironing was up to date. Ticking off her tasks satisfied her.

Today she added checking in on Michael to the list. Their friendship changed after his move into the Lodge, but she supposed that was normal. His life was so complicated and hers so predictable, but she missed the time they used to spend in the garden. She hoped given time and the adjustment their closeness would return because he made her laugh and listened to her describe the ups and downs of her marriage without judgement.

She rang the doorbell of The Lodge and took a step back. Her watch read 10am, not too early for a visit to someone who didn't have a job.

"'Lo." The door opened revealing a stocky man with receding light-brown hair.

"Is Michael in?"

"Are you from the hospital?" The man fidgeted on the doorstep.

"No, nothing like that, I'm just a friend of his. Said I'd pop by today. He's expecting me."

The man breathed out and opened the door a fraction more.

"It's cos I keep thinking they're going to take us back."

"Can't imagine that's going to happen. The government need to show their new initiative is a success." She smiled at him. The world was less about people's lives and more about the money that service provision cost the authorities. "Is Michael in?"

The man pointed to a metal board on the wall beside him. It listed the names of the five residents, two women and three men. Michael's name appeared midway in the list, the metal sign flipped to the right indicated he was at home.

"Do you know where his room is, or do you want me to get him for you?"

"First floor, end of the corridor?" she asked and continued into the building before the man could reply.

The halfway house made her nervous. Its design, though adapted from a normal residential building, still housed the markers of a hospital with its muted, clinical colours, the notices on the walls, the signing in and out board. A mental health nurse was assigned to the building and regularly visited to talk through any difficulties residents were encountering in their transition from the closed, regulated environment of the unit to the freedoms of living in the community.

Clare flicked the switch, turning on the lights before proceeding up the narrow staircase to the first floor. Reaching the top, she straightened her dress and checked her hair was in place. It was a trick taught by the bank who liked their staff to be meticulously dressed, in case a stray hair affected the ability of cashiers to bank cheques, dispense cash and help the public with their enquiries about loans, mortgages and overdrafts.

"Hi, Katie." Clare looked up from appraising her appearance to see Rebecca emerging from Michael's room, dressed in an oversized white t-shirt just covering her bum, hair dishevelled.

"It's Clare. Is Michael in his room?"

"He's asleep. I wouldn't disturb him. He's had a restless night."

Rebecca twirled her hair around, smiling as she spoke her final sentence.

"Oh, I see. Thing is I promised I'd visit today. Is he alright? He seemed particularly low when I saw him yesterday. I'm a bit worried."

The smile slid from Rebecca's face like cheap mascara in a rainstorm.

"He's fine. I'm looking after him Katie."

"My name is Clare and I'm sure you are, but I'd like to see him all the same."

"I wasn't going to mention this, but perhaps it's better that I tell you after all."

"Tell me what?" said Clare, putting on her best dealing with a difficult customer voice.

"Michael thinks you are annoying, always popping round, wanting him to do this and do that. He said you behave like a pathetic, nagging wife."

Clare stared at her, stunned by the viciousness of her words.

"I think it would be better if you don't see him again, don't you?"

"I, I... Michael wouldn't have said anything like that. He's not like that."

"But he did and from what he's told me it's the truth. You should go now. Michael's got me, I mean got me." She pulled up her t-shirt, laughing as she displayed her nakedness.

"Okay, I get the message. I'm going. Whatever he thinks, please tell Michael I was here. I won't come again unless I hear otherwise from him."

Clare pushed her rage down into her stomach. She clinched her fist to stop herself from slapping Rebecca. As she walked downstairs the light went out.

"Bye Susie, look forward to not seeing you again."

Clare swore under her breath and hurried through the lounge to the front door and out into the unseasonably mild day. Once in her car, out of sight of the house, she allowed herself to cry, letting angry tears trickle down her rouge infused face. How could Michael think such things about her? Was she overbearing? It was the sort of thing Steve would throw at her in the heat of an argument. She thought he said it out of frustration but now she wondered if there was some truth in his words. She had seen Michael a lot since he was discharged into the community. If Rebecca was speaking the truth she couldn't see him again. The idea triggered further tears and she pulled a pack of bank standard issue tissues from her bag and blew her nose. Nothing she could do now. With still a couple of hours before her shift started but not enough time to justify going home, she started up her car. Right now, there was nothing she wanted more than some retail therapy, nothing more that is than a hug from Michael.

Chapter Nineteen

WINSTON BANGED his fist on his desk and winced. Rubbing his bruised hand with the other he looked around him. This was his office, he'd earned his place here and now it was put at threat by a grievance against him made by a miniature Welsh librarian. He sensed the snooty woman from HR enjoyed handing over the letter summarising the complaint and summonsing him to a meeting that afternoon. "Threatening behaviour? Bullying and harassment? No woman has ever accused me of anything like this before. My record is unblemished."

"Did you want something Winston?" said Marilyn, calling through from the other side of the office partition.

"I am... talking...to myself." He said through gritted teeth. "Get me some coffee, the usual." That would keep her out of his hair for a while and when she came back he would give her a complicated list of jobs to do, the boring complicated ones.

Ignoring the pile of work on his desk and the unread emails in his inbox, Winston flipped through his social media apps searching for any new posts from anyone related to the library. Included on his list were Begw, Trevor, Sketch and a bunch of old people who shared results of quizzes that told them who they were in a past life and that they were going to marry and get pregnant in the next twelve months. He flitted from search to search, noting with a snarl that Trevor and Begw had made many of their posts unviewable to people not connected with them online. Begw had also shared a series of posts about kettles through the ages.

"Bloody boring," he said to the screen of his smartphone. He enlarged one of the images with his fingers remembering that his mum once had a similar kettle when he was a teenager. He swiped away the nostalgia with a humph. Continued searching led to the discovery that the girl called Sketch still maintained a public profile, sharing her persona and all her thoughts online with anyone who wished to drop in on them. She shared everything: photos of her surrounds, pictures of her friends, random thoughts and views on politics, world news and local events. He leant back in his power chair, threw his arms wide and laughed. How naive was this Sketch girl? he thought. With all the information she shared he was sure to be able to pin some dirt on Begw and do away with her petty and unfounded grievance.

A tentative knock interrupted his thoughts.

"Winston," Marilyn walked in and presented him with an over-sugared coffee. "Anything else I can help you with?"

He smiled slyly, flexing his hands out in front of him before taking the drink from her.

"As it happens there is. What have you found out about that girl, Sketch?"

"Plenty, she's an oversharing teen but mostly harmless. Asks lots of odd questions like she's from space or something."

"What sort of questions?"

Marilyn took her phone from her pocket and brought up an electronic file she kept to log her research on Winston's stalking targets.

"Lots of 'why' questions? The sort of ones little kids ask. For example, 'Why do people who have money not share it with those who don't? Why do countries have borders? Why is the sky blue?' She answered that one herself after doing a bit of googling. Don't think she's doing anything wrong. She's just not street wise. I kind of like her."

Winston frowned and sat up straight.

"Like her? She's part of the gang of misfits who are trying to destroy me. They've got no idea what being in charge and having to make decisions is like."

"Errr, no, sorry Winston, I guess not." Marilyn bit her lip. "Is there something specific you want to know?"

He took a swig of his coffee and coughed it back up as it went down the wrong hole.

"Sometimes, I think they put poison in these things. Look for anything about where she's doing something illegal, particularly if Begw is involved." He spat out the librarian's name like she had personally spoilt his coffee drinking experience. "Get it to me before you go home. This is urgent now. I'm off for a cigarette."

Marilyn nodded assent and returned to her desk, putting aside plans to write a thousand words of her draft by the end of the day.

Chapter Twenty

SKETCH AND TREVOR were in the middle of binge watching episodes of 'Britain's Top Vlogger' when Matt rang the doorbell of their fifth floor flat. Half eaten packets of Mexican cheese flavoured snacks, cans of fizzy pop and the more wholesome and cheaper glass of tap water favoured by Sketch covered the coffee table. A lack of income constrained her intake of sugar and as her only money came from Jackie and Trevor she became creative about not spending it.

"Alright Matt," said Trevor. "Want to join us?" He shuffled up on the sofa leaving a dip the sofa cushion.

"Seen it. Gets really good in the next episode. Actually, can I have a chat with you, Sketch?"

"Sure, want to go for a walk? The Heath will be looking lovely in the sunshine."

"Okay, we might as well enjoy the amazing weather, the sun will be gone by tomorrow."

Sketch kissed Trevor on the cheek and jumped up from the sofa.

"Let's go."

Hampstead Heath, one of the lungs of London, stretched for seven-hundred and ninety acres. Older than the buildings surrounding it, the green space and forests encompassed within its boundaries had borne witness to changes enforced by the passing of time. As Sketch and Matt sauntered through its manmade pathways and conserved trails many others did the same. The Heath was popular with families, couples on dates, dog walkers and runners, the throngs of the capital escaping concrete structures and pollution. It seemed to Sketch the warmth of the sun transformed the smells and sounds, bringing out the best of them against a background of birds soaring across blue skies. She smiled to herself.

"You must be pleased Social Services have backed off," said Matt.

"I'm so relieved. Now, Jackie is safe, I get to go to college and there's the chance of an apprenticeship." She high-fived Matt before spinning around.

"So, what's up?" said Sketch as they parted to avoid a bounding terrier chasing a dog twice its size.

Matt regarded her. "It's difficult."

"Most things are but I've found if you talk about them enough someone will have an answer, maybe not the one you want to hear but an answer all the same."

He chuckled.

"That's just it, I think I know the right answer but whether it's right for me or not I'm not sure."

Sketch stopped and gazed around enjoying the sensation of the sun beaming down on them.

"You should tell me about it now, while the sun is shining. It's easier to be positive when the weather is brighter."

"Aw, Sketch, that's what I love about you. You can always see the positive side of things."

Sketch blushed. Matt giving her a compliment still had that effect, although she'd long since come to terms with the fact they were only friends. It was for the best, she would be returning to the Core just as soon as the computer was fixed.

"It's about uni."

"I thought you were going to take a year out and reapply after saving some money?"

"I was or at least it's the decision which made most sense for Sammy and Ashling, but now I'm not sure. At school, everyone was applying, and it made me think what if, what if I didn't have Sammy."

"Matt," said Sketch, eyes wide open. "You can't say that. You can't say that about Sammy."

Matt dropped his eyes to the ground.

"I love Sammy, wouldn't be without him really I wouldn't but you can't deny life would be easier, everything would be easier if he wasn't in the picture. So, I started to look at courses."

"You did?" Sketch thought about it. It didn't do any harm to look and technically Matt was correct, without Sammy in the picture he would be free to do what he wanted. Except Sammy was part of his life.

"Yeh, and I might have filled out my UCAS form." Matt bent his head and focused on his fingernails.

"What?"

He shrugged. "I didn't even know if anywhere would accept my applications as I'd missed the deadline, but some places have."

"Oh," said Sketch, not sure how to respond.

"I'm just not sure not going is the right thing to do. It will be hard for a few years, but I can have a job and study at the same time. With a degree I'll get a better job."

"What's Ashling and your mum have to say about it?" Sketch knew Ashling would love the chance to go to uni, but she couldn't support herself and Sammy, neither did she want to depend on the kindness of Jackie forever

"Yeh, Ashling's not one hundred percent on it."

Sketch raised an eyebrow.

"Ok, so she went mad and I can see why but I also need to do this. It's hard to explain, I just do."

"And your mum?"

"She thinks I'm being selfish, that Ash and I should be able to go to uni but not until we've got Sammy into school and settled."

"It's not that long 'til then, couple of years or so."

"And until then? Am I supposed to work at a chicken shop or a call centre making next to nothing?"

"Maybe, it's somewhere to start. A bit of work experience will look good on your applications."

"Is that something you read online Sketch? After all, what do you know?"

Sketch stiffened. Tears welled up in her eyes.

"I can't believe you said that, Matt. I might not have had the life you have but I try to understand what it's like, how you must feel."

"I'm sorry. My head's a mess, don't know what I'm saying."

She chewed on her lip, willing the tears back into her body despite Matt's apology.

"Come here," he said. He pulled Sketch towards him and put his arms around her.

"Hug?"

"Hug."

The power of a human hug always awed Sketch, the touch of someone's skin, the heat emitting from their body and the sense you mattered enough to someone to make them want to hold you close. She snuggled into Matt's chest.

"Sketch?"

"What?"

"You better not be wiping your nose on my t-shirt."

Sketch laughed, sniffed and, pulling away from Matt, swiped a tissue from the pocket of her trousers, using it to blow her nose, fix her face and dispense of the last remnants of sadness.

"Maybe it doesn't matter that you applied. You don't need to make a decision yet. If you get in you can always defer. It's months to go yet and some unis have subsidised creches."

"You're right. You're normally right." He looked at her in a way which made her turn her eyes away.

"Shall we get an ice cream?" she said.

"Top idea, genius girl."

Sketch's stomach lurched.

Chapter Twenty-One

MICHAEL STEPPED into a room of faces, some familiar such as Sister Rosy and others he couldn't attach names or memories to, which he took to mean they were meeting for the first time. They sat around a tessellation of tables, pushed together to allow them all to form a semi-circle. At the length of the tables nearest to them was an empty chair.

"Hello Michael," said an efficient looking woman in her late thirties, dressed in an off-the-peg suit and shirt unbuttoned to reveal sun-blemished skin. Michael didn't understand how he knew the extent of her UV damage, but he did. However, he stopped short of warning her about the rising risk of skin cancer and perils of a sunbed tan. She stopped short of being orange.

"Take a seat," she smiled, gesturing towards a uniform plastic chair. He surveyed each of the faces, noting their smiles. He smiled back. Rebecca had told him to smile, to agree with them and keep them smiling.

"They'll smile anyway but you can tell which ones are real and which are fake, plastic, medical smiles," she had said.

"I'm Trudy Mostrum and you've met most of my colleagues, but we'll do a quick round of intros just in case."

The mental health professionals, social workers and housing manager stated their names and roles putting faces to the professionals listed in the letter he had received a couple of weeks ago.

He smiled, this time not because Rebecca advised it but because they seemed nice.

"As you are aware, we're here to review how you are getting on, look at progress and decide whether or not you need further support." In front of her sat a pile of papers which she shuffled into order before reading from the top one.

"This is a summary of the feedback from your mental health in the community team. According to them and everyone around the table you are making good progress. Living outside the unit seems to be working for you, but tell us Michael, how are you finding things?" She put emphasis on you and he saw Sister Rosy smile at him and nod.

He gulped, wishing it was the weekend and he could be out clubbing with Rebecca, be alive and part of the world rather than facing a panel of people who knew he didn't fit into the mould of his skin.

"It's been good, good but hard as well."

A few heads nodded as he spoke.

"And," Trudy Mostrum scanned her notes. "Tell us about what you've found challenging."

Michael scanned through the answers he had rehearsed and stored in his mind. Then he froze. This question didn't feature on his list. His hands began to sweat, and he felt his breath punch its way out of his lungs.

"Err, I don't know."

"There are no right or wrong answers Michael, just take your time and say what you think."

Sister Rosy pushed a glass of water across the table towards him. He grasped it between both hands mingling perspiration with the globules of water condensing on the outside of the glass. He didn't know how to answer. How could he tell them that he didn't feel like he belonged, like he was in the wrong skin, a borrowed body which one day he would have to return?

Then there were the flashes. They came in the darkness of night when the house spoke in creaks, with hisses of electricity and fridge gases. They crept up on him when surrounding noise reduced to a minimum, they assaulted his senses. They were like the pulses he experienced when clubbing but without the unadulterated joy. Instead, came variations of monochrome flashes like sheet lightning, lights popping on and off and bulbs dimming without switches.

Always they were light and dark. There was never any colour. He had read in a magazine article that many people dreamed only in black and white, seeing the world as dogs do. Perhaps the flashes were like that, daytime dreaming or perhaps they were a malfunctioning of his brain, the same malfunctioning wiring which had resulted in his hospitalisation and the wiping of his memories. Yet the occurrences of flashing, the black and white disco lights, didn't scare him. He felt they belonged to him, and that somehow each pulse of light held a clue, an answer to the puzzle of his origin. What frustrated him was that the clues led nowhere, he couldn't decode them. It was like waking from a dream with the details of all you have experienced in the night dissolving, dripping away through the gaps between your fingers.

"I sometimes don't know what to say to people," he said swallowing his words as quickly as he mumbled them.

"It's part of the human condition," said his designated mental health nurse. "And you get better at it the more you do it."

Michael smiled. Smiling was one of the things he could fake. Around the table pens scribbled and ticked boxes with biro blue and black ink.

"I know. Not having a garden is hard. I miss the garden from the unit."

"Well, given your love of nature and how you demonstrated a skill for it we have a proposal for you."

A cardboard file appeared in front of him, a sticky label positioned top centre read "Werrington Garden Centre and Cafe". He looked from it to the various members of the panel.

"What is it?"

"It's a garden centre, a place they grow and sell plants to the public."

Michael looked puzzled. "I know what a garden centre is. What's the proposal?"

"It's simple. A job as an assistant gardener. There will be an interview but you're the only one in the running. You've made an excellent start, progressed well and the next step is employment."

"With a job you'll be in control of your life, truly independent."

He flipped open the folder, taking in the photocopied images of different sections of the garden centre and friendly smiling staff members. He'd not given much thought to a job, but it made sense, and if he had chosen a job wouldn't it have been this one?

"And if I have a job can I move out?"

"Yes, in fact you'll have to," said the orange skinned Trudy.

"What Trudy means is moving on from the Lodge is an important part of your recovery and return to the community," said Sister Rosy interrupting her colleague. Trudy pursed her lips.

"Thank you for that nurse. Michael, the job is in North London. We'll help you find somewhere to live and you will have some money to help you relocate. It really is a good package. This sort of thing doesn't come up often."

"London? I can't move to London."

"We know it's scary but there'll be a transitions team there and your new GP will be sent all your information."

"I'm not going."

"Michael, this is your best option: a job you'll enjoy with support to settle in, and London is an exciting city."

He couldn't smile and didn't want to frown so settled his features into a bland neutral position.

"Do I have to go? Can I not stay where I am?"

Around the table, eyes swivelled about in a form of silent communication he couldn't interpret. As the vocal silence continued he focused on his breathing, a technique acquired in the unit which helped to still the panic battling to take hold of his mind.

"Michael?"

The voice brought him back to the room and to the faces staring at his. He scanned each of them, noting their eyes and assessing if their concerns were real and if so what was behind them. He settled his look on orange Trudy, convinced hers was fake.

"Yes."

"We can't make you take the job or move to London."

"Oh. Well, I'll stay where I am, where I feel safe."

The Housing Manager shifted in his chair.

"Cards on the table Michael, your stay at the Lodge has been longer than planned and the room is now needed for other people coming out of institutional care."

"Then I'll move out."

Chapter Twenty-Two

BEGW JONES FACED A DIFFICULT DECISION. The fight to prevent the library being closed and turned into an overpriced chain convenience store kept her awake at night. The anti-wrinkle eye cream she swore by no longer stopped the shadows from setting up shop under her eyes. She'd resorted to applying cold green tea bags to them three times a day; they didn't work except as a deterrent for Trevor, whose chatting disrupted her thought processes. The thinking bit irritated her. Logic allowed her to get through life without irksome problems but this time a persistent moral dilemma decided it wanted to get in on the act. She activated her phone with voice controls, requesting it play her voicemails.

"Hello Begw, it's been an age, hasn't it? Look, I'll get straight to it. There's a job going here with your name on it. If you moved here it would give us a chance to give it a go, give us a proper chance. London might only be seven pages on an atlas but it's not close enough. It's ten thousand miles away. Bell me back if you're interested. I still love you."

She played the message back three more times before removing the tea bags from her eyelids and shoving her phone under a pile of essential items in her bag.

"Why do you do this to me, Deborah?" she said out loud to an invisible person only she could see in her mind.

Nothing would please her more than to pack her compact flat into boxes, ship them to the new world and hop on a plane to a new life, with a chance to rekindle a fledging love that hadn't had the chance to burn to its brightest. Yes, it was risky, but she didn't care about that. London would always be here if she needed to come back, but that wasn't it. How could she leave the library now? At a time when everyone had banded together to save it and believed she wanted it as much as them. Begw didn't think she was indispensable, but one less member of staff to make redundant would make it much easier for Winston to implement his plans to get rid of the crucial services the library offered to the community. Didn't his mother read to him when he was small? She humphed.

The door creaked open, revealing Trevor who, noting the tea bags next to the sink, sidled up beside her.

"Things are getting busy out there again. Shame we don't have Sketch with us anymore. Can't she come in as a volunteer?" he asked.

"Isn't she at college?"

"Starts next week, with a whole load of weird teenagers with suspect hair, spots and enthusiasm."

"Well then, she can't, can she? Ask her to pop by on Saturday though if she's free. As a volunteer, you read the memo about not taking on any more staff."

"Sketch brightens things up, don't you think? Everyone loves her."

Begw smirked. "If I didn't know better, I'd think you were turning into a heterosexual.

"Moi? Never. A cute man is all that turns my head, but Sketch, well she's like the sister I never had. And I'm her gay bestie."

"And what does that make me?"

"Her second gay bestie." Trevor ducked to avoid the copy of the Evening Standard Begw threw at his head.

"You owe me a panad for that comment. Don't forget..."

"Only half a teaspoon of milk," he interrupted.

Begw smiled to herself. Having someone who could finish your sentences gave you a glow. She wished Deborah could be the one to make her feel warm inside, but so many people needed her here and letting them down didn't appear on the list of things to do before she died.

"And I'll have some of those chocolate hobnobs you've hidden away behind the herbal teas no one drinks," she added before checking her newly chopped fringe was still straight and heading back into the busy throng of the public area of the library.

Trevor saluted as she left. He put the kettle on, wondering what was getting her down. Perhaps the threat of closure had finally become too much for her. The idea of unemployment scared the hell out of him, but it might not come to that. Plenty of time to be glum when it came to be having to sign on for benefits. Or it could be something else. Despite working with Begw for years and having gone to the pub with her on uncountable occasions he knew little about her. She lived alone, was fussy about quantities of milk she added to hot beverages, but her friends, relationships, loves and heartbreaks remained a secret. Social media offered Trevor the odd glimpse into her likes and dislikes, but aside from a plethora of photos of unusual road signs and kettles she posted nothing clue worthy. Trevor didn't mind. Begw's enigmatic persona made her the perfect boss, and what he did know was that she always had his back. No matter what.

Chapter Twenty-Three

MICHAEL SHOVED JUMPERS, socks, underwear and assorted clothing into the second-hand suitcase he'd arrived at the Lodge with. He abandoned his usual compartmentalised neatness in favour of the 'scrunch it up and throw it in' method. His head spun. Where would he go? What would he do for food? Money? Where was Rebecca? She could advise him what to do. As long as he stayed close to her, life would be okay. She got him, and when they merged his world lit up. She laughed at him when he used the word 'merge' to describe their love making.

"Never heard it called that before. The strangest of things come out of your beautiful mouth," she said, kissing him again. "Where did you hear that?'

But Michael didn't know. It was just another item to add to the list of things which marked him out as different from everyone else, so he ignored it and continued with the kissing, apparently something he excelled at.

With his meagre belongings packed, he sunk down to the floor, wrapped his arms around his calves and buried his face on his knees. Clare flashed into his thoughts. He swiped her from his mind. If she cared, she would have been in touch by now. Her silence told him everything he needed to know. He chose to sleep. Sleep, even with the dreams, recharged him, helped him to be more logical in his responses and decision making. On waking, the world would be as new, even if only for a few seconds.

As he swaddled himself, a repeating word blinked into his mind, 'sketch'. He flipped his eyes open and grabbed for his bag, from which he extracted a pen and notepad and began to etch the word into the page, decorating it with swirls and flowing lines, filling the blank off-white space with the contents of his head.

A high-pitched laughed tripped Michael out of his trance.

"There you are. What happened at your review?"

Seeing Rebecca made his heart vibrate. He leapt up and pulled her towards him.

"They want me to go to London."

Rebecca looked up at him, "For training?"

"No, to live."

Rebecca's mouth twisted downwards into a frown, her eyes welling up with tears.

"But how? Why? What about us? They know about us, right?"

"Of course they do," said Michael. He didn't mention Rebecca to the panel, but his psychiatrist and crisis team knew he'd started seeing someone. "They don't listen, do they? Don't worry, I'm not going."

They stood facing one another, gripping each other's hands. Michael took a deep breath, "But I've no clue where I'm going to live. They'll make me leave here."

Rebecca began rubbing his arm and twisted her hair around her nose with her other hand. He melted when he watched her playing with her blonde locks, but his breathing remained laboured; the trick of being in her presence failing to calm him this time.

"I can't believe they've done this. It's inhumane. We're in love. They are saying this because they're old. They can't remember what love is like. They go home to their box houses, with their boring husbands, wives and bratty kids. My parents are as bad. Oh!" she exclaimed.

"What?"

"My parents, they're going away for the summer. Got a house in Spain and I'm not invited. So," she gleamed.

"So?" asked Michael.

"So, we can live in their cottage in the country. You and me, the whole place to ourselves."

He frowned, "Like the old people who go home to their box houses?"

"Us? Never us."

He swept her up, her feet elevated above the carpet and spun her around, just avoiding her legs colliding with the functional furniture filling up the room. In that moment, it seemed possible that everything could be fine, everything could be perfect. Him, Rebecca, a house and a chance to become whoever he wanted to be.

"You mean it?" he asked as they toppled down onto the bed.

"Like I've never meant anything before. Let's get packed up and go now." She pointed to his bag. "You're done, so help me get my shit together and get out of here."

Michael brushed stray hairs away from her face, smiling. "Do you want to check with your key worker?"

"No," she said laughing. "My review's next week. I can still go. They're only going to tell me to leave anyway. It's my parents' house and I've got loads of meds. Plus, we've always got party pills."

"But,"

"No buts," she said stopping any further talk with a kiss, a kiss Michael felt surge through his body, filling him with a multitude of coloured lights. Rebecca was his drug of choice.

Within an hour, Michael and Rebecca removed the traces of their time at the Lodge, sweeping clothes, books, crumpled receipts, posters and unwashed crockery into bags, bins and sinks. In a final sweep of his room, Michael spotted the plastic herb pots lined up on the window sill behind the partially closed curtains.

"Have you got something I can put these in?" he asked Rebecca who stood in the corridor with her suitcase and shoulder bag.

"Leave them. The cottage has a garden. You can grow anything you want there."

"But," he began. She made a face resembling a sad dog, putting on the giant puppy eyes for extra effect.

"You heard what I said about buts. Come on. I called Andy. He's going to pick us up. God knows his car is better than getting the smelly bus with all those weirdos."

"I guess."

Michael looked again at the plants on his window sill grown from seed. This was a fresh start, so he supposed leaving them behind was the right thing to do. Growing their love trumped some rosemary and parsley.

"Let's go then," grinned Rebecca.

Chapter Twenty-Four

"WHAT SHOULD I WEAR? Jeans, dungarees? Wellies?" Sketch's head popped into the space between Trevor's bedroom door and its wooden frame, followed by a hand holding a collection of clothes hangers and a pair of spotted rubber boots.

"You have wellies? You have wellies in North London?" Trevor peered over his Egyptian cotton clad duvet, rubbing his eyes and squinting at the walking wardrobe.

"When I searched online I found lots of people wearing wellies for gardening and the internet says they're good for festivals too."

Trevor stretched his gangly arms above his head and yawned.

"Are you going to a festival?" he asked, smirking at his flatmate.

"No, to college, the gardening course starts today."

"Get rid of the rubber boots. You won't need them. The British summer is upon us, and although Britain isn't known for its endless days of blue skies and sunshine, I doubt you'll need wellies in North London."

"Really?"

"Yes, really. And besides which, they are an affront to fashion."

"Like socks and sandals?"

"Exactamundo."

Sketch placed the boots outside the door and transported the remaining selection of clothing to the topside of Trevor's duvet cover.

She held up pair of red, cotton dungarees. "Here's my dilemma. Because today is my first day, I want to make a good impression, but I also don't want to ruin an outfit with mud."

Trevor leafed through the pile of clothes before pulling out a stripy black and white t-shirt and skinny jeans. "Here you go," he said placing it with the dungarees. "That'll do you."

"Thanks, Trevor. What would I do without you?" Sketch spun around holding her outfit against her body pretending to dance with an exciting partner.

"Oh and, Sketch."

"Yup?"

"Ask them college hotties for some overalls."

On arrival at college for her first session as a human student, Sketch posted online, highlighting her location, tagging in friends and a torrent of hashtags about positivity, college life and growing stuff in cities. Underneath her excitement, Sketch's thoughts swirled, remembering her last experience as a student. Back before her transformation into human form, she'd been a trainee computer energy, and not a very efficient one. Distractions, her crush on Matt and an inability to understand human behaviours resulted in her temporary exile from her home in the Core to learn how to be a human in the human world. The proceeding collapse of the computer meant Sketch couldn't return. Thousands of energies played a vital role in making technology work. This was one part of scientific knowledge human research had so far failed to discover. Inco, the One, Virder and a host of other energies might be transformed, living their lives as humans, dogs or ceramic pots, but she could still stick to her brief to learn, to be the best human she could. Distractions were a thing of the past, Matt was now just her friend and her grip on all things human vastly improved.

Phone deposited into the inner pocket of her bag, Sketch navigated her way through the corridors of the Victorian section of the college building, ending her journey at room G22b, marked on her information sheet as the horticulture department. A first glance through the small, glass panel in the door suggested she was the first to arrive. After straightening her clothes and practising her favourite smile, she rapped on the green wooden door, noting a fleck of paint flake off as she knocked.

"Come in."

Entering the classroom, Sketch filled with a glow of sunshine. She sensed this place fitted with her. This time, she would excel at studying. In front of a desk piled high with textbooks and charts and scattered with seed trays stood a woman with golden red hair, strands of which caught the light, which made it appear alive.

"Welcome to Gardening 101. I'm Clare Smith, your tutor. What's your name?"

Sketch grinned. "I'm Sketch."

"Sketch?" The coloured drained away from Clare's face.

"Oh, I know. My name's a bit strange but you get used to it quickly," said Sketch. "Actually, it's Sketch Smith. Maybe we're related."

"Sorry, I didn't mean anything. Smith is a very common name, isn't it?" Clare paused. She retrieved a tablet from under some dirt-smeared papers.

"As I thought, you're not on the list. There's a Skeeter. Could that be you?"

"I guess, I registered, filled out all the forms, but things can go wrong with online things. They can go really wrong."

Clare gestured towards a bench on the front row. "It's not a problem. I'll check with admin later. Have a seat."

As Sketch slid onto a seat the door opened and a straggle of young people rambled into the room. She sighed as she viewed their mismatch of clothing and saw that none of them wore wellies on their feet. *Thank goodness for Trevor,* she thought, looking down at her red baseball shoes.

Sketch scanned each of her contemporaries, looking for clues about who they were. Of the assembled students, two were female. The only other girl in the room chose a seat at the back. She wore purple boots laced up to her knees, black shorts and an oversized white t-shirt emblazoned with the slogan, "Frankie says relax." Her mid-length hair with rainbow strands scattered throughout brightened her pale skinned, round face. In front of her, sat a thin black teenage boy. He pulled a green spiral-bound notebook from a branded backpack, and sat up straight as a pole, face front. Another two boys fiddled with smartphones, nudging each other in the side and sniggering at their respective screens. The final group member stood towering above everyone in the room, like a Swedish giant. Sketch had read a short story in which a journalist discovered the existence of giants living in plain sight in South London and began to question whether or not it had been fictional.

Clare Smith clapped her hands.

"Welcome to Introduction to Gardening 101 - B786a. That's the course number. Write it down now as you'll need it later for the raft of paperwork the college requires. Now, I've met one of you already but let's have a round of introductions." She peered around at the assembled students, her eyes settling on the girl with rainbow hair. "You go first. Tell us your name, your motivation for doing the course and your favourite plant.

"Hi, I'm Mae, Mae Fountayne. I chose this course because I want to grow colourful flowers. I've got a thing about, well bright things. As you can see," she said, bumping up her hair up. "Plus, my nan loves them, and she needs help with her garden."

Sketch grinned. Mae knew how great older people were. Perhaps she could introduce Mae's nan to the library campaign group. Her attention turned to the front row as the slender, earnest looking boy began his personal elevator pitch.

"My name is Dwayne. We, my family that is, don't have a garden. We live in a flat on the thirteenth floor."' "Unlucky for some," said one of the other teens. "We live on the thirteenth floor," continued Dwayne, his serious expression sprayed with extra firm hairspray to his face. "We don't have a garden, but I want to grow things. My fingers are feeling the green." A snigger came from across the room, but Dwayne remained unfazed, folding his arms and sitting up even straighter in his plastic chair.

"Thank you, Dwayne," said Clare. Her eyes journeyed from the enthusiastic teenager whose fingers danced in front of his face to the pair with smartphones glued to their hands.

"And you two?" she asked.

"We need the credit, Miss. I'm Craig and he's The Grapevine."

Clare didn't laugh. "The Grapevine eh?"

"Yeh, my mum dumped me with this stupid name, Marvin. Like that old singer bloke, Marvin Gaye. She loves him, plays "Heard it through the Grapevine" all the time, so I is the Grapevine."

"And your favourite plant?"

They looked at each other and sniggered.

"Don't mind a bit a weed, Miss."

Sketch absorbed everything she could about the conversation. Humans still intrigued her, with their variable behaviour and the way they twisted language and broke its rules. Lost in her thoughts, she failed to notice it was her turn to introduce herself until she sensed a gaggle of eyes boring into her.

"Oh, hi. Hi everyone, I'm Sketch. I'm here because I have to do some education or training or something or my guardian will be prosecuted. All the IT apprenticeships are full for now and gardening is the only thing I could start immediately." The faces of her tutor and course mates stared at her.

"And for the green growing things. Nature is wonderful, isn't it? My favourite plant is a cactus; they are prickly, good at surviving without much help and suddenly burst into beautiful blooms. They remind me of humans." Sketch beamed. Gardening 101 rocked.

One boy remained, the tall blonde one Sketch imagined to be a Swedish giant. As he spoke, his northern accent discounted this possibility.

"Hey, I'm Harry. We moved down from Manchester last month. I plan to go to uni and study horticulture. Thought this would help towards my application, along with my A-Level courses."

Sketch's brain whirled around. She thought she recalled chatting to a northern boy called Harry a few months back. He mysteriously disappeared without a word. *He couldn't be the same one, could he?* she thought.

Chapter Twenty-Five

THE SOUND of wailing scratched through the air as Michael stepped through the front door of the cottage. He raced to the kitchen, following the animalistic cries to their place of origin. Rebecca stood surrounded by pieces of broken glass, plates and mugs, her face smeared with black mascara and eye pencil mingled with tears. Her face radiated pain. Her hand held tight around the neck of a bottle of red wine. He approached her, tiptoeing around the fragments of kitchenware, unsure what to do.

"Rebecca, what happened? Are you okay?"

He reached out to her, but she shrunk back from his touch. Had someone hurt her? The shop was only a half a mile away and it was only twenty minutes since he'd left, sent to buy some hummus to eat with the carrot sticks and pepper chopped for dinner, or supper as Rebecca called it. When he'd left, she smiled at him, seemed happy, contented. Now she looked broken, defeated and somewhat wild. Her eyes pleaded with him but didn't tell him what to do to fix her, and he suspected anything he tried would be a sticky plaster to her mind.

"It's okay, it's going to be fine," he said, holding his hand out and nodding towards it. "Let's get away from the glass, to somewhere safe." She shuffled, hunched up like a ball of negative energy, contained but ready to explode, towards him. He panicked, breathed and tried to recall the procedures used by staff at the unit to subdue people who were having an episode, a moment as some of them called it.

He guided her out of the fitted kitchen, into the small, cosy living room, a room in which he felt a sense of calm. With no agenda other than to take away Rebecca's distress he gently lowered her onto the sofa, positioning her legs along the length and laid her head on top of a plump cushion. Kneeling next to her, Michael stroked her hair away from her forehead and began to hum the tune to a song Rebecca had been playing on repeat during the three weeks of their stay in the cottage.

"Sorry," she sobbed, wiping snot from her face with the sleeve of her cardigan. "I can't."

"You can't what?"

"This. All of this. You, me, life. It's too much. Why are you here? I'm mad, crazy, mental, why are you with me?"

Michael stared at her. "But nothing's wrong. Everything here is fine. I'm with you because we love each other." Inside he ran Rebecca's questions through the cogs of his mind. If he could find the answers she would work it out. Words had power. He'd learned that when he first appeared in the world, in Clare and Steve's living room, in his time at the unit when he sat with his silence, learning to speak and listening to the way people manipulated situations with their words.

"I love you, Rebecca."

She shook her head, her hair flying around as when she danced to a grunge track.

"No, you don't. You just think you do. And who are you anyway? No one knows where you come from. God, you don't know where you come from."

"I can't find the words, the ones you require," he said. Rebecca threw her hands up.

"There you go again with your freakiness. Required? What's that supposed to mean? People don't speak like that, not normal people."

He jolted backwards, her words stinging his face.

"I'm sorry. You're having a bad day. Come here." He drew her close until her head nestled into the curve of his neck. He stroked the length of her hair, smelling its lemon freshness mingled with her scent of her anguish. He didn't want Rebecca to feel this way, yet he was lured by the idea he could make her better. The sun shone through the windows of the cottage and he wondered if this was what it was like to have a family? Someone who held you close when you were sad, wiped the tears from your skin and still loved you when your face displayed the signs of upset.

"Becca?" he asked, dropping a kiss on the top of her head.

"Ummm," she said, the word muffled by the side of his neck.

"Did something happen? Did someone," he paused. "Did someone hurt you?"

Rebecca snorted, and a raucous laugh took the place of her previous anxious cries.

"Hurt me, no, but my olds rang. They're coming down tomorrow. Some nosy bloke from down the road told them we were here. Well, what he actually said was he'd seen a couple of squatters camping out at the cottage and did they want him to call the police?"

"What did you tell them?"

"That it was me and a mate from school. Andy in fact. They like Andy."

"Oh." Michael shrank into himself. He gazed at the floor, not wanting to meet her eyes. He failed to understand what he'd done wrong.

"They wouldn't get it. You, me, the mental thing, and they would freak out if they put two and two together and realised the naked living room guy and my boyfriend were one and the same."

"I suppose."

"Look, it's not all bad. I know I lost it earlier but I'm fine now. We'll give Andy a ring and see if you can stay at his, just until we sort something else out. Oh, and we should have a party tonight. Make the most of the last night in the cottage."

She hugged him with a quick squeeze before jumping up to the kitchen to use the phone. He stared at door and pondered the sudden transformation in Rebecca. He was in love with a whirlwind.

Chapter Twenty-Six

MICHAEL'S EXPERIENCE of house parties, as of most things was limited, but he was surprised the word spread so quickly and that cars full of people he'd never heard of let alone met descended upon Rebecca's parents' country cottage. They arrived with carrier bags full of crisps and those new snacks from the States which were so moreish that once opened were impossible to put down. Cans of lager, bottles of spirits and ready mixed concoctions with names such as 'Mad Dog' filled up the work surfaces on the kitchen and scattered themselves on the floors next to sofas, on stairs and bookcases.

He scanned the room looking for Rebecca, who had gone in search of some guy who had promised to bring them E. Her earlier upset had disappeared as she ran through phone numbers in her address book, laughing with friends when she called, telling them to bring everyone with them, saying it would be the party of the year. He found the switch in her character odd, but a long hug and her rejuvenated smile impressed upon him the importance of the here and now. Tomorrow they'd be apart, sleeping in different beds in houses across town from each other back in Hartington.

"Watch it," said a boy with baggy jeans and hair which flopped round his face, as Michael bumped into him.

"Sorry, have you seen Rebecca?"

"Who?" The boy shouted above the sound of the Happy Mondays.

Michael leaned in closer to his face, "Rebecca, have you seen her?"

"Dunno, who's Rebecca?"

Michael sighed and squeezed his way between a couple snogging on the stairs. At the top of the stairs, he froze as a vision of another party, in another time hit him with a violence that forced him to the ground. The pulses of light returned as he watched the ensuing party scene as an onlooker. He saw a group of teens who appeared to be similar in age to himself and the gang drinking, smoking and making out around the cottage. There were differences between the two groups. The clothes worn by those in his mind varied from the real-life fashionistas, and he noted many of them held devices which they repeatedly pressed with their fingers. Whatever they were, they each had their own but still shoved the screens of the devices into the faces of their friends, resulting in laughter, expressions of disgust and raised eyebrows.

From the throng appeared a tall thin, blonde girl, with eyes full of upset, tearing through the room towards a back door, followed in seconds by another girl calling out to her.

"Sketch!"

This single word jolted him back to the present and the retching of someone vomiting in the toilet. Michael's head whirled. The vision revealed vital clues to his past, but he couldn't join up the dots to show the final picture. He took a deep breath in through his nose and pushed the air out through his mouth. Sketch, Sketch was a name, not a thing, not related to drawing, but the name of a girl, a girl with blond spiky hair and she was his friend. He grinned. Sketch was a person and he remembered something from the time before he woke up in Clare's living room all those months ago. And if he could remember one thing, if Sketch was real, then perhaps he could remember it all. To do that meant finding her, but with a name like Sketch, it couldn't be that hard, could it?

"What you doing sitting there?" asked Rebecca, appearing above him, pulling her hair to one side of her neck. "There's a banging party going on and look what I found." On her open palm balanced a couple of pills.

"Wanna get happy?" she said as she slid down next to him. Before he could reply, she handed him a half-drunk can of lager and an E. He kissed the top of her head. Everything was going to be okay.

"I'm already happy," he said. "I remembered something." He peered at her, waiting for a response.

"But imagine how much happier you'll be when you take this," she said, pushing the pill towards him again.

"Ummm. I'm not sure I want one."

Rebecca pursed her lips and glared back at him. She withdrew her hands and her offer.

"I don't know what's wrong with you tonight, but you're not going to spoil it for me by being all weird again. I'm off to find someone who enjoys my company."

"But I..." Rebecca didn't give him time to explain before flouncing off down the stairs. He heard her put on her happy voice, a pitch higher than normal and bouncier than sounded natural, at least to him. He sighed. He should follow her, shouldn't he? As much as he loved her, right now he would rather pull apart the details of his memory to see if he could make sense of it. He drew off into the master bedroom, finding his notebook on the side table, a habit left over from the unit. Crossed legged on the bed, he jotted down everything he could recall about his mind's earlier disclosure; writing it down made it real, concrete and not a figment of his imagination.

On closing the notebook, he looked over to Rebecca's side of the bed to check the time on the clock radio. The display read three minutes past twelve and he realised he should return to the party, catch up with Rebecca, maybe take an E, if it wasn't too late. As he turned towards the door he spied a used condom on the carpet.

Why did people think it was alright to do things in someone's bed at a party? He tore a sheet of paper from his pad and scooped up the offending object, parcelling it up ready for the bin. Rebecca's parents would be unimpressed to find out what her friends had been up to in their bed.

Chapter Twenty-Seven

EACH MORNING, Sketch got up early, made her breakfast of sausage sandwiches with tomato ketchup, cleaned the kitchen and read up on the content of the previous day's lesson at college. Gardening was fascinating and reminded her of the essence of energies and their lifecycles. How a tiny seed transformed into a green shoot poking out of the earth, or into flowers that closed their petals down at night and came alive again each morning with the rising of the sun. To Sketch, such change was beautiful. It reminded her of how things can be rejuvenated, brought back to life, and perhaps by studying hard and learning the principles of plant energies she could find a means of applying them to the broken-down computer.

Sketch adored being a student. College opened up a new group of friends whose acquaintance helped her growing understanding of what it was to be human. Although living the life for herself, Sketch never felt she had a proper grasp of what it was like to be born as a baby and grow up in human form. A data package, downloaded before she left the Core, provided much of her knowledge about the world and the way people behaved. The rest, like loss, grief, sadness, rejection and hope, enthusiasm and love, she'd learned the hard way - by experiencing them herself. London and the people she met provided the perfect lessons for a trainee computer energy who now knew she could help make their lives easier when she returned to the Core. That is, should she manage to restore the computer to a working condition.

As she walked along the busy corridor to her classroom, Sketch listened to the noises of education, sniffed in the smells of the college, young people's deodorants, aftershaves, perfumes and sweat mingled with the lingering scent of floor cleaning fluids and high-pitched chatter. She grinned, amazed by the sights and sounds she encountered every day.

"Tomatoes!" shouted a piercing voice into her ear while a pair of hands covered her eyes. Sketch wriggled away from her captor, her heart racing. What on human earth did they want from her?

"Get off me!"

"Whoa, what's eating you?"

With her eyes free and her breathing returning to normal Sketch realised it was her friend Mae, the one with the multi-coloured hair from class.

"Sorry, but you shouldn't attack people like that," said Sketch attempting to be smiley again.

"Just messing, innit," Mae shrugged. "Sometimes you seem like you're from another planet."

"Tomatoes? What about tomatoes? Aside from them being red and fruity." Sketch's taste buds tingled at the thought of biting into a fresh, yummy tomato. Mae pulled a packet of seeds from her duffle bag and waved them at Sketch. Before Sketch could comment, a hand snatched the packet from the air.

"Harry!" exclaimed Mae. "Give those back." Harry replied with a grin. He winked at Sketch and shook the soon to be tomato seeds around.

"If you can catch me," he said speeding off towards the boys' toilets.

Mae scowled with arms folded against her chest.

"That boy is exasperating. I think he likes you though."

"Me? What makes you think he's interested in me?"

Mae tapped the side of her nose.

"I just knows," she guffawed. "Nose, knows, you get it?"

"Is that a joke?" asked Sketch. Despite having improved on the comedy front since becoming Trevor's flatmate, she didn't always pick up on the humour cues.

"Doh! But I can tell. I have the sense, like gaydar but for straights, an that boy got the hots for you, Sketchy."

Sketch felt the familiar warmth shoot up her cheeks accompanied by an inner glow and some wriggling in her stomach. She linked arms with her classmate and dragged her down the corridor leading to their classroom. She pushed thoughts and questions about Harry from her mind.

"Now, what was it you were saying about tomatoes?"

"They're my chosen project. Figure they'll be well on the way to being actual plants by the time the holidays come around. Plus, I'll be able to take them home and pick them whenever the hungry mood takes me," said Mae. "What about you? What's your project about?"

Sketch reached into her bag and dug out the seed picked up from the DIY store in Tottenham Hale on a visit with Jackie.

"Kale?" asked Mae. "What the hell is Kale?"

"Kale is one of the super foods; super good for you, super robust and super easy to cook. I read it's becoming the trendy green to eat."

Mae snorted. "I'll believe it when I see it. Let's go liberate my tomato babies from your boyfriend."

"He's not my boyfriend!"

"Whatevs."

The session sped past. Harry left without a goodbye glance, grin or a cheeky wink at Sketch, confirming her view that he had no romantic interest in her. It left her feeling lower than she understood why. To cheer herself up she invited Mae for a posh coffee in the college café, where being a student meant a sizeable discount on the high street price. A regular in the cafe, Sketch shared greetings and smiles with fellow students and the resident baristas.

Over a triple shot caramel latte with a topping of rainbow sprinkles, the pair talked about hair. Mae appraised Sketch's signature blonde spikes. After much umming and ahhhing, poking and measuring with her fingers Mae sat back and shared her thoughts.

"Your hair is distinct like, but have you never been tempted to go rainbow, like me?"

Sketch rolled her eyes upwards as if to look at her hair.

"No, not really. Do you think it would suit me?"

"Not only would it suit you, it'd look sick." Sketch beamed inside, having learned the alternative meaning of the word sick and not making a fool of herself by asking what anyone would want to have hair which resembled vomit.

"I could do it, you know? Watched them do it loads of time at the salon when I did work experience."

"I did my work experience in the library," said Sketch, proud of her time spent working with Trevor, Begw and the Silver Surfers.

"Boresville. Now back to your hair. Do you fancy it?"

"I suppose," said Sketch. Change was part of being human and trying new things had worked well for her so far. But her hair was special to her. She'd chosen it in the Core and her human avatar meant a lot to her. *It's just hair, right?* She thought. *What harm can it do to add an incey wincey bit of colour?*

"Okay, let's do it."

Chapter Twenty-Eight

THE DAY AFTER THE PARTY, the cottage reeked of stale beer and cigarettes and everything within its walls resembled a party hangover. Ornaments, rugs and books were displaced, soil knocked from plant pots, and half-drunk cans and bottles hidden in nooks and crannies. Michael had stopped short at an E the night before but drank more than could be called responsible. His stomach lurched and churned as he said his goodbyes to Rebecca.

"Are you sure you don't want me to stay and help to clear up before your parents get here?"

Rebecca kissed him on the cheek and twisted her hair around her fingers.

"No, it's better they don't meet you yet. Anyway, they already think the worst of me. Me throwing a party and wrecking the joint won't come as a surprise."

"I'm going to miss you."

"Me too but remember it's just a few days. Nothing can stand in the way of you and me." She hugged him, squeezing his skinny frame.

"Andy's waiting in the car, so you best get going."

He kissed her again, trying to breath her essence. If he inhaled it, he could keep a part of her close.

"See you soon gorgeous Rebecca." He walked away with a glance over his shoulder. Without her something would be missing, but then something was always missing. Not knowing who he was, his past, who his family were, or if there was anyone out there searching for him. There'd been no mention of him on the missing people lists held by the police and voluntary agencies, but that didn't mean there wasn't a chance a relative was looking for him.

"Come on mate," said Andy through the window of the red Ford Fiesta. Michael bundled his belongings into the backseat of the car and strapped himself into the passenger seat. The interior of the vehicle looked as unkempt as the cottage post-party and was occupied by the same scent of stale tobacco. Andy lit up a fresh cigarette further upsetting Michael's senses, but he managed to keep his face neutral, grateful to the guy for letting him stay for a few days.

"How's it all going with you and Rebecca?" asked Andy. He tapped the steering wheel, drumming to an invisible beat as he drove down the narrow country lane.

"Everything's good." Michael thought it best not to go into detail about their relationship; Andy didn't seem the type to talking about feelings with. The more guys he met the more he realised they had an unspoken code amongst many of them about what it was appropriate to talk about. What a girl looked like fitted but more emotional stuff like falling in love was a no no.

"She can get a bit lairy when she's off her happy pills."

"Oh, she's still taking her medication," replied Michael.

"You think? I'd take bets on her heading back to Crazyville." Andy wound down the window, stubbed out his cigarette on the in-car astray and threw the dog end out of the car. The sudden waft of fresh air gave Michael much-needed respite from the stale smoke as he considered Andy's words.

"She promised me," he said, both to himself and to Andy. "She's taking them."

"If you say so mate, if you say so."

Michael didn't know whether he could trust Andy, but he had

faith in Rebecca. Someone who loved you like she did couldn't lie to you about such an important matter, could they? It wasn't logical.

Now he was cigarette free, Andy took the opportunity to speed up, taking corners at a pace which alarmed Michael. He gripped the handle on the side of the door and inhaled large gulps of air in an attempt to quell the nausea building up in his body.

"Mate, you look green. Do you need me to stop?"

Michael shook his head and grimaced. He couldn't throw up in the car so set his eyes straight ahead and steeled himself for the next bend.

As they travelled back in the direction of Hartington, the hangover symptoms began to subside and with their departure Michael's memories of the night before started to sharpen. Out of the mindfog emerged a memory of the vision he'd experienced on the stairs, the one with the girl called Sketch. He also remembered it was all written down and his notebook was stuffed in his bag in the boot of the car.

"Err Andy?" He said. "Any chance we'll pass somewhere I can go to the toilet?"

"There should be a Little Chef in a few miles. We can stop there, get some scran too. Fancy some chips, me."

"Chips sounds good." Deep fried strips of potato were, Michael had discovered, one of Rebecca's favourite foods. It turned out that deep frying even the blandest foods added a special something to them, and once you sprinkled on salt and poured on dollops of tomato ketchup they were delicious. Michael had acquired a taste for them.

As the vehicle pulled into the car park of the UK's famous roadside diner, Michael found his energy returning. His notes from the night before would shed a light on his past, and he could set about making a plan to find the girl.

"I'll just fetch my bag from the boot," he said.

"Your stuff will be fine in the back. No one's going to break into this beauty." Andy rubbed the dashboard and grinned.

"My wallet is in my bag. I'm paying. That's the least I can do."

Andy threw him the keys and stepped out of the car.

"In which case, here you go. I'm going to have a smoke. See you in there."

Relieved not to be offered another cigarette, Michael walked round to the boot and popped it open. Inside his bag, sat his notebook and the key to his future life.

Chapter Twenty-Nine

THAT AFTERNOON AFTER COLLEGE, Sketch had arranged to meet up with Matt. With his A-level exams looming, studying took up much of his time and Sketch missed his company. Her new friends were lovely, but they were different from Matt, who she'd known her whole human life. At college she shied away from conversations about her earlier life because she couldn't explain she came from the inside of a computer. Although they all carried around smartphones and tablets they had no inkling their devices worked because of the conscious light-infused energies which resided within them. Everyone believed microchips, circuit boards and electricity made things function, but without the presence of energies nothing worked. With Matt she could talk freely. He still scratched his head when she mentioned the Core, but he believed what she told him.

As well as missing spending time with Matt she wanted to show off her new hair, transformed into six different colours by Mae, who had forgotten to wear plastic gloves when applying the dye resulting in a murky smudge all over her hands. Sketch's hair, however, brought joy whenever she caught sight of it in a reflective surface.

They arranged to meet at Matt's house in Tufnell Park where

she found him in the dining room, with books and papers splayed across the expansive wooden table.

"Whoa, Sketch - did you catch a rainbow? It looks...well it looks colourful?" said Matt.

"You like?"

"It's different." He examined her hair from different angles, taking in the different hues, viewing it through an invisible camera with one eye shut. "Sure, the colours are kind of you. Bright, sunny, out of this world."

She laughed. "What are you revising for?" Sketch slid onto a chair next to him. She picked up a text book with a picture of a mushroom cloud on the cover and flipped through the dog-eared pages.

"The Cold War. You know about that?"

She nodded. "That's a bit of the data download that trans-ferred." Before her transformation from computer energy to human, Sketch had undergone a process downloading vital information about the world she was about to join. But not all the data had synced meaning she often found gaps in her knowledge which resulted in quizzical looks from people who found her answers confusing or eccentric.

"Time for a break," said Matt. "I'm guessing you'll have a cup of tea?"

"Yes, please," said Sketch. She loved the ritual of a cuppa, a habit acquired during her time spent living with Matt and Jackie. Tea from a teapot with a dash of milk poured in the mug first, remained her favourite drink, but she was happy if the teabag went straight into the cup.

She gazed around the room, taking in the familiar sights of the piano, the sofa onto which she collapsed when she first arrived from the Core. Things looked a little different now. Children's toys and paraphernalia belonging to Sammy and Ashling gave the place a different feel, one of a younger, more hectic family home.

"Here you go," said Matt, presenting her with a mini teapot and matching mug.

"Wow, where on earth did you find this gorgeous, perfect thing?"

"A new gift shop's opened on Fortess Road. Mum and I saw it and thought of you. You like it then?"

"I love it, thanks a hundred times, then a hundred times again."

Sketch leaned over and gave Matt a brief but happy hug. "Where is Jackie?"

"She's on a date, I think. But don't tell her I told you. She thinks I don't know but given the amount of time she put into getting ready, there's got to be a man involved."

"Or a woman," said Sketch as she poured her tea into the new mug.

"I guess," said Matt. "But I don't think mum's into women."

"How can you tell?"

"I can't but I'd know, wouldn't I?"

Sketch didn't answer, leaving Matt's question hanging. The pair drank their drinks, Matt having opted for a can of fizzy pop to feed his sugar addiction.

"How's thing's going with the Core rescue project?" he asked.

Sketch sighed, "It's not. I'm stuck for answers and to be honest, I'm avoiding the obvious."

"Which is?"

"That the computer is beyond repair. If it's unfixable then all the energies will have been automatically transformed."

"Oh. Do you have any idea what? If that's what has happened, what would they have transformed into?"

"They could be anything. Except," she paused, examining the dregs of her tea.

"Except what?"

"Except if they knew it was going to happen. Then Operation Evacuate would be put into play. The energies would disperse in an orderly manner, based on their history, performance, seniority, that sort of thing." A small glimmer of a smile began to take seed on Sketch's face. "They could even be humans, they might be here, in your world!"

"Really? In human form? Like you?" Matt stared at her.

"Oh yes, they could be anyone. In which case, I must start searching for them, because they'll need help adjusting."

The idea that her fellow energies might be in the same world as her filled Sketch with a renewed sense of hope. She'd been focusing all her efforts on rebooting the elements of the computer which housed the Core and its inhabitants, but the likelihood of them still being there was getting lower as time went by.

"I get what you're saying Sketch, but I don't see how you'd even start trying to find them. There are billions of us people living on the planet. They could be anywhere from here to Timbuktu."

She saw from the look of concern on his face, that he was worried about her, but from Sketch's perspective finding her fellow energies presented an achievable challenge.

"But you see Matt, they know I'm here, so they will be trying to get in touch with me too."

He returned her smile, grabbed some clean sheets of paper from across the table and put them in front of her.

"Come on then. Let's make a search plan."

"I could kiss you," she beamed, clamping a hand over her mouth as she realised what she'd said. He glanced back at her and their eyes connected in a way which turned her to jelly. She shook it off, convinced it was a figment of her imagination rather than a mean-ingful moment. Matt leaned in and quickly pecked her on the cheek and then pushed the pen and paper towards her.

"Okay, let's start with who's likely to have been transformed into human form," she said, hoping her face didn't look beetroot and Matt couldn't see her shaking.

"What about your friend? Inca? Is that his name?"

"Inco. Yes, he was still new to the Core, but his performance ratings soared above many of the other qualified energies. Oh," said Sketch, ideas whirring around in her brain. "There's this boy at college called Harry. At first, I thought he might be a giant but he's not from Sweden, but Mae says he likes me. He could be Inco!"

Chapter Thirty

ANDY'S FLAT gave off a distinctive smell; one of young men living in close proximity where laundry and dishes went undone for too long. Michael's attempts to change this to a friendly odour failed and went unnoticed by Andy who, Michael assumed, was content with his surroundings and their whiffs and unpleasant scents. Keeping the flat clean not only proved difficult but an obstacle to what he wanted to be doing, tracking down the mysterious girl from his vision. With only a first name, albeit an unusual one, to go by Michael decided to start his search at the local library. Each day, he set out into town and requested the microfiche on which copies of daily and weekly local newspapers were stored. He began the process of methodically searching them for signs of the name Sketch.

If only there was a more efficient way to search for people, he thought. *Something like one of those new computers but one housing all the information you might ever need.*

However, microfiche was what was on offer to him. As well as searching for Sketch, he also noted mentions of his appearance in the local and national press and conducted a scan of newspapers in the period before he turned up in the Townsend's front room. He found nothing from before that date and forced himself to stop look-ing. The process saddened and frustrated him to a point that it jeop-ardised his enthusiasm for the hunt for Sketch.

On a telephone call to Rebecca, he attempted to explain why finding the mystery girl was so important to him, but she seemed put out by his actions.

"I don't see why you're making such an effort to find some random," she said.

"She might know things, about me that is. It gives me something to do to stop missing you as well," he said. He did miss her, her voice, her touch, sharing stuff together. He didn't have anyone else to talk to. Andy chatted about parties, clubs, drugs, girls he fancied, but he showed no sign of wanting a deep and meaningful discussion.

"When can I see you?" asked Michael, gripping the handle of the payphone.

"Not for a bit, babe. My olds think we should stay in the country a while longer. It's not what I want, but best to keep them on side."

When they'd lived in the Lodge, Rebecca's parents hadn't seemed to show an interest in her re-joining the family, so now they were supporting her to do just that, Michael was reluctant to push anymore. He didn't want to be the sort of guy who'd stop her getting closer to her parents.

"It won't be for too long, babe. Then we can have a proper reunion, just you and me and maybe an E," she added.

"I suppose so."

The sole good thing about Rebecca being away was that he could continue his investigations into Sketch without annoying her further. As he shifted through news stories finding nothing related to Sketch, he thought back to their phone call. The tone of Rebecca's voice sounded different, a little too high-pitched, over the top, after he'd explained his reasons for the search for Sketch. Perhaps it was the phone, conversation didn't flow as well when you couldn't see the other person's face or observe their body language.

"Michael?"

A familiar voice stirred him from his introspection. Turning from the screen, he found himself facing Clare.

"It is you," she said, smiling the smile he liked, the one that matched her golden red hair.

"Hi," he said before recalling they'd not spoken for what seemed like years.

"Where have you been? I went to the house, but they said you moved out. No one would tell me where because of confidentiality and whatnot."

"We went to the country, Rebecca and I," he replied. "I'm back now."

"So I see. What are you up to?" She nodded at the microfiche scanner.

"I'm researching. There was a moment," he paused not knowing how to best describe his vision and guessing it might not be wise to tell her all the details about the party when she might not approve. "A memory came back. Just snippets, but it provided some clues."

"How fantastic! Look if you don't have to be anywhere why don't we go to the new cafe on the high street and get a coffee? I hear they do a great line in the Italian stuff."

The microfiche would still be there the next day and with no plans to call Rebecca he agreed. He'd missed Clare.

The smell of ground coffee beans tickled Michael's nose as he held the door for Clare. Not much of a coffee fan, he allowed himself to be convinced to try cappuccino. Clare giggled.

"You've grown a moustache," she said, leaning over to wipe chocolate sprinkled milk foam from his face with a paper napkin. "How are you?"

To tell or not to tell. Sometimes it was better to let slip a little of what you felt, the uncontroversial bits not primed to explode in the recipient's face and make them angry, sad or worried.

"I'm okay." He scanned her eyes. A glint in them told him this wouldn't be enough. He'd not cracked the worried bit.

"I'm staying with Andy, he's a friend of Rebecca's, for a few days. But like I told you, I am remembering things, a girl. And, and here's the thing, her name is Sketch."

Clare nodded. "Really? Is it an actual memory or more like a dream?"

"A memory, I wasn't asleep when it happened. And I know it's real. I can feel it here," he said, tapping his left fist in his chest close to the position of his heart.

"Sorry, it's just I've heard of people coming off their medication and having strange side effects. As long as you are okay, that's all that matters. And you are remembering things."

Michael winced but the smile growing on Clare's face and sparking in her eyes reassured him and his heart rate stabilised.

"Tell me about it, about her. Maybe I can help, "she said.

He recounted his memory. As he talked, he wondered what was happening in Clare's life, how her mother was, if things were going well with her burly husband Steve. He made a mental note to ask her later.

Chapter Thirty-One

WINSTON HID across the road from the library, attempting to look incognito behind a group of people milling around the bus stop. Chain store coffee in one hand, he wondered if this was the ideal time to start smoking again. He pondered the options but ruled it out on the basis of it being too expensive and him having gone off the smell since quitting. Besides which, since the government imposed a legal ban on smoking in public places in 2007, having a puff on a cigarette this close to the boundaries of a bus stop was against the law. Instead, he pulled his phone from his pocket and scrolled through his social media accounts for any trace of new posts or mentions of Sketch. Asides from some photos of fledgling plants and a torrent of likes, comments, purple love heart emojis and teenage babbling nothing significant popped up on his screen. Days and days of weird questions, pictures of cats, small children playing with toys and blasted 'keep our library open' campaigns had Winston in a burning rage and prompted him to change tactics. If online stalking wasn't working, why not the real thing? Only he preferred to think of it as detective work. A misspent childhood filled with TV cop shows from the States, provided a backdrop for his revised plan, but without, he thought, a comedy sidekick to show off his clever brain and stunning good looks.

Across the road, unnoticed by the Head of the borough Library Service strolled Sketch and her friends from college.

"Sketch, that bloke who's been following you is over there," said Mae, peering at Winston over her shoulder. Sketch sighed, turning to check who it was.

"He's the guy who wants to shut down the library. Can you imagine it? A world without a place where anyone can come and borrow books, read magazines, see their friends, apply for benefits?"

"But why's he following you? asked Harry, who Mae was convinced fancied Sketch. Sketch thought otherwise.

"I'm not sure. Perhaps it's because I'm friends with Trevor and Begw and part of the campaign to keep the library open."

"Don't get it," said Harry.

"There's plenty you don't get," said Mae with a snort.

"Ha ha," he fake-laughed, shoving his scrunched-up face in front of hers.

"Get off!"

Sketch pushed between the pair and linked arms with them.

"Hey, you two, let's get inside before he recognises me."

Inside the library, Mr Moore readied himself to convene the meeting, shuffling leaflets and checking notes on his iPad. Sketch introduced her college friends to him and to Trevor, Begw, Jackie and Matt. She winked at Matt as he said hello to Harry. After their conversation, the idea that the energies from the Core were alive and well in human form had taken root in her brain and grown like knotweed. Every time Harry said something which might lead her to think he might be one of the energies or Inco in particular she noted it down on a virtual post-it on her phone.

She cornered Matt after the meeting, behind the crime fiction section. "What do you think?" she asked, standing on tiptoes equalling him in height.

"He seems like a bloke, a teenager. He's a bit up himself, isn't he?" Matt shrugged.

"There's nothing different about him?"

"I wouldn't know what to look for. After all, I didn't guess you weren't a human, did I?"

Sketch sighed. Maybe Matt was right, she was chasing a dream. Her former friends could be anywhere or anything by now. A pig in the city farm, a UPVC window, a vibrant colour energy making up the spectrum of a rainbow. Why would they be in human form?

"Hey now," said Matt. "What have you done with my Sketch? My Sketch would be seeing the sunny side, putting on a happy face, looking for clues, not slouching behind a bookcase." He tipped her chin up.

"What do I know? After all I'm only a human and not the world's best human either."

She managed a nod and took a deep breath while orchestrating an internal spin in her mind, in an effort to increase her lightness. It used to work for her in the Core so why not out here?

"You're right. We can make a list of questions to ask him which will help us to know if he's an energy or not, even if he isn't aware of it himself."

Without thinking, she grabbed his hand and pulled him away from the stack of books and back to where Mr Moore lingered with some of his fellow campaigners. She'd never held a boy's hand before, not unless you counted Sammy and he was a just a tiny tot. Her body lit up, filled with a soothing yet stimulating source of power. Matt's hand was warm, smooth (he didn't do a lot of gardening), and holding it made her tingle. Reluctant to withdraw from this new sensation but conscious of what people, and Matt himself, may think, she took her hand away and rubbed her nose.

"Okay," she said, avoiding eye contact, a little scared of what she might see in Matt's eyes.

"Yeh, okay. I'll see you later in the week then." She nodded again, today she was good at nodding, as he picked up his bag from the information desk and made for the door. What had she done? What would he think of her? *Stupid, stupid, stupid,* she thought. *I'm such a female.*

Deep in a tornado of thought, Sketch jumped when a pair of hands extinguished the light from her eyes.

"Mae! You've got to stop doing that."

"Nah, you love it," said her friend. "Guess what?"

"What? You got an A for your tomatoes?"

"Nope. Guess again."

"The coffee shop at college is having a half-price sale so we can buy more than one hot, sugary drink a day?"

Mae gave a little dance as she replied. "Still not right. I'll give you a clue. It's about a guy, a guy who likes you. His name begins with H and ends with Y."

"Harry?"

"Spot on sister. The girl has got it. Don't raise your eyebrows. He's been asking about you? I think he's going to ask you on a date."

"You do? I'm not sure he's my type."

Mae flung her hands out. "Jeez girl, have you seen him? He's everyone's type. Dumb as but fit to look at."

"Thing is Mae, I'm not sure I want a boyfriend. What with college and the campaign and trying to fix my computer, I can't think where I'd find the time for dates and hanging out.

"And snogging," added Mae. "I bet you my best tomato plant he's going to ask you. And you better say yes."

Sketch considered what her friend had said. After making a giant fool of herself over Matt it would be good to have someone to distract her. Matt was never going to want her, not when he went for girls like Britney. Maybe she would say yes, if, and it was a skyscraper sized if, Harry asked her out. A date would provide the perfect opportunity to suss out whether or not he was human.

As she left the building, giggling with Mae, she noticed Winston still stood in front of the dry cleaners. She gave him a wave before jumping on a bus back to Trevor's flat.

Chapter Thirty-Two

DESPITE SPENDING as much time in the library as its opening hours allowed, scouring the archives of local and national newspapers and records, Michael failed to find the faintest trace of a girl called Sketch. At Clare's suggestion, he instigated a search of birth, death and marriage records, but with only a first name to go on, albeit an unconventional one, a lack of information halted his request before he could get started. Perhaps this mystery girl was the result of a drug induced hallucination. Someone at the party could have spiked his drink, but somewhere in the back of his mind Michael believed she existed. When he recalled the vision, the girl remained tangible, like he could touch her, like they connected in some way. And Sketch was his first remembered word, the one he played on repeat during his time in the unit. It seemed unlikely his mind would attach a word associated with art, drawing, pencils and charcoal to the name of a young woman. This lack of logic encouraged him to believe Sketch was indeed a human being and not one he'd made up or dreamed into being. So, where was she?

In the spare room of Andy's flat, by the side of the grimy mattress Michael slept on, laid his notebook, a phone card and a pile of change. The coins and card were for phoning Rebecca.

Andy's phone didn't make outgoing calls and Michael had become frustrated waiting in for Rebecca to call so each day at six o'clock, when the call rate became cheaper, he walked to the nearest phone box and dialled the number for her parents' cottage. For the last few days, her parents had fobbed him off with excuses: she's not here right now; Rebecca's resting; or she's gone out for a walk, the fresh air's good for her, you know. They were polite but firm. Each time, he left a neutral message, asked her to call him and left Andy's number. When he awoke on day four and Rebecca still hadn't called he began to worry. What if something had happened to her? Maybe her parents didn't give her his messages? Perhaps she couldn't use the phone because her levels of distress were too high.

He hauled himself out of bed, dressing from the pile of neatly folded clothes in the wardrobe-less room, in a uniform of long-sleeved band t-shirt and baggy jeans Clare had bought him from the summer sales. He tiptoed through the house, ignoring the unwashed dishes in the sink and the beer cans by the overflowing carrier bag which doubled as a bin, careful not to wake up Andy. He couldn't face a conversation with his flatmate.

The nearest public phone box to the flat was littered with rubbish, numbers scribbled on bits of paper and ads for adult services, and the glass panels were decorated with spray can graffiti tags. Michael wondered at the human need to mark their territory when they lived on a planet rich with resources and beauty. On stepping inside the phone box, Michael threw his head back and laughed.

"Of course, out of order. My life is out of order."

Michael walked in the direction of the centre of town, knowing the chances of finding a functioning call box was greater there. He didn't believe in a god or the universe controlling events, the science he'd read in books told him otherwise, but he wished things were simpler. If he stripped back what he wanted it came down to living a good life, being happy and having Rebecca share it with him. And friends, friends like Clare. He'd like lots of them. He could find a job, in a factory or picking veg on a farm, get a place to live with

Rebecca. But his search for a window into his past put barriers in the way of any kind of simplicity.

In the bus station, two out of three of the phones were operating. Michael auto-piloted his way through the phone card connection procedures and punched in the number of the cottage. It rang. He steeled himself, thinking through what he might say when he spoke to her, but the ringing continued until it connected to an answering machine.

"Hello, this is the Saunders family. Patrick, Mason and Rebecca. We're not able to come to the phone right now, so please leave a message, we know no one likes leaving a message but go on. Wait for the beep." The voice stored on a tiny cassette on distant machine sounded upbeat, but Michael replaced the receiver in its cradle before the beep came. Leaving a message meant getting home before she called back. He might miss her. Better to stay put and call every fifteen minutes until they returned.

He located a plastic seat not far from the row of phones, wriggling to make himself more comfortable as the bus station didn't allow for the luxury of padding. There he sat and watched, observed people come and go, with bags of shopping, children, pushchairs, hopes and dreams for the day, for their lives. In between his musings and people watching, Michael took the fifteen paces needed to reach the phone boxes and fifteen steps back again when the phone continued to ring through to cottage's answer machine. He continued this on repeat until six-thirty, before giving up. Hungry, thirsty and despondent, he returned to the flat, worrying about Rebecca and missing her more than ever.

"Mate, where you been?" asked Andy, slumped on the sofa watching a video of people inflicting violence on one another. "You been with that posh bird?"

Michael frowned. Sometimes he couldn't understand what Andy meant. He looked around the living room which remained unchanged since the morning aside from a takeaway pizza container filled only with crusts and what appeared to be anchovies on the floor next to Andy.

"Posh bird? Who do you mean?"

"That Susan or whatever her name is."

"Clare, and she's not posh."

"Whatever you say, mate," said Andy, lighting up a cigarette and offering the packet to Michael.

He shook his head. "No, thanks. Has there been any calls for me?"

"Nah, quiet as a sleeping babe here today. It's Sunday, everyone's recovering, coming down and such. Were you expecting one?"

"From Rebecca. She said she'd call."

"Becs? You'll be lucky. She had it large last night. Went off with some tall dude, all hippy an all that." Andy turned back to his film, pressing play on the remote control as Michael snatched it from his hand.

"What do you mean? Rebecca's at the cottage with her parents."

"Is that what she told you? Sorry, mate. Rebecca's been back in town for days. Trade off with her folks. She's promised them she'll go back to college and keep seeing the shrink."

Michael stomach lurched. His hand leapt to his mouth to prevent him throwing up over Andy.

"Here, you're as pale as a pale thing." Andy edged over, making room on the sofa and gestured for Michael to sit next to him. Andy continued speaking but Michael's focus slipped in and out, picking up bits of it, key words, snippets of sentences, things he didn't want to hear, things he didn't want to be true.

"...Went with that bloke at the party...thought you knew...asked me to let you stay...not the first time she's done this."

He twisted his head to look at Andy's eyes. His face, his pupils, his body language indicated he was telling the truth.

"But she loves me," whispered Michael.

"Rebecca don't love no one. She's too messed up. Don't take it personally. It's not you, it's her. You want a beer?"

**** ornamental break What?

The phone rang. Clare jumped from her bed. Calls at this time of night always brought bad news. With adrenaline pushing to the corners of her body, she picked up the receiver.

"Hello?"

"Clare, it's me, I mean it's Michael."

"Are you okay?" she asked, rubbing some sleep from her eyes. "It's late."

"I'm sorry. I'm fine. I just wanted you to know I'm leaving."

"Leaving? Going where? Why?" Her sleepiness prevented her filtering her responses, instead words popped from her mouth.

"To London. I spoke to my care team. The job they offered me, it's still available."

"That's great news." Clare's feelings didn't echo her words. She didn't want him to go. "When are you leaving?"

"In the morning. I wanted you to know, so you wouldn't worry."

"Okay."

"I'll be in touch. Once I'm settled. Night Clare, and thanks."

"For what?"

"For being you in a world full of people who aren't you."

Clare stared at the phone as Michael ended the call, leaving her listening to the dial tone and the sound of Steve's snoring from the bedroom.

Chapter Thirty-Three

WHEN SHE FIRST TRANSFORMED FROM a computer energy into a teenage human girl, Sketch landed in the living room of Jackie and Matt. As such, she considered their house to be her home. In a similar way that goslings imprint to their mother, Sketch imprinted to the house. Nestled in a side street away from the bustling Fortress Road, the Victorian terrace retained its sought after original features but had been updated over the years to include reliable indoor plumbing, electricity and central heating.

The hub of the house was in the area previously allocated as a basement. Former owners had gutted it and built an extension out towards the back garden, which was at a lower level than the front. It provided enough space for a small kitchen; a dining area furnished with sufficient room for a large table, and an adjacent living space with sofa and a piano. Upstairs were bathrooms, bedrooms and a little used, more formal, front room. Since Ashling and Sammy joined the household last December, Jackie had given it to them as private space, but they usually opted to spend time in the basement with Jackie and Matt.

As Sketch waltzed into the house she shouted hello. The thickness of the walls meant someone could be talking on one floor and not be heard by anyone else. She poked her head around the door of the front room but found no one there. It looked tidy aside from a few toys which had fallen from Sammy's box. The stairs to the basement met the corridor at the far end. On reaching them, Sketch began to pick up the sound of voices. She grinned. Ashling and Matt were downstairs. What better than two of her favourite people in the same room and if Sammy was there she could sneak in an auntie cuddle. Although not an actual auntie to the little boy, Ashling had given her the honorary title, telling Sketch she saw her as family. An auntie cuddle could blow away the saddest of moods, however, today Sketch was bouncing, enthused about the growth spurt of her kale and her not-a-date date with Harry.

"Lovely friends, it's me," she beamed as she rushed down the narrow staircase, forgetting she'd once nearly knocked herself out falling down it. She stopped and looked from one to the other as they both glared at her and then back at each other.

"Hi Sketch," said Matt, not looking at her. His face looked thunderous and matched Ashling's hostile visage.

"Hey," said Sketch. "What's up with you two? You look like you've lost a million pounds and found a penny." Neither laughed at her mixed up saying.

"Ask him," said Ashling, her mouth twisted, and arms folded tightly in from of her. "He's the one who wants to wreck everything."

Matt sighed and put out an arm towards her. She shrugged him off.

"That's not what I'm doing, if you will just listen."

"Listen? I've been listening and all I'm hearing is you going, 'I want, I feel, I think'. Really, Matt? Can you hear yourself?"

Sketch froze. She should do something to intervene but her track record at fixing human problems was hit and miss. Anything she might say could make things worse, so she decided to combine the learning from her time in physical form and the data she'd been given in the Core. She jumped between the two, holding them apart.

"What are you doing, Sketch?" asked Ashling in a voice Sketch thought could be mistaken for an angry dog bark.

"Stopping you fighting. It works in films, every time."

Matt removed Sketch's hand and stepped away. "We're not hitting each other. This isn't TV, Sketch, this is the real world. You should understand that by now." He stomped off up the stairs leaving Sketch stung by his words.

"Forget it," said Ashling. "He's an insensitive oaf. Why are you still even friends with him?"

"He's my friend?" Sketch's tentative answer hung around as she searched for a way to break the tension. She decided on a hug and flung her arms around Ashling; hugs were up there with sausages as her favourite human things. She felt Ashling's mood transform from a rigid anger to a softer, calmer demeanour as her friend's muscles relaxed into the cuddle.

"I'm sorry, it's been a long day and life is hard enough without Matt making it more complicated with his crazy ideas," said Ashling. "Ignore me."

"Why would I ignore you?" asked Sketch. "You're sad and they say talking about it can help. Tell Auntie Sketch all about it." She noted a tiny smile appear on her friend's face. "Oh, but first I need a proper auntie cuddle. Where's Sammy?"

Ashling nodded at the sofa. "Having a nap. Can't believe he slept through all that."

The pair squeezed onto the sofa, one at each end with Sammy between, like a couple of bookends.

"What's Matt said this time?" Sketch kept her voice low so as not to waken her pseudo nephew.

"You remember how he told me he was going to find a job and take a year out before going to uni?" Sketch nodded. "Well, he's only accepted an offer to go away in September." Sketch lowered her eyes.

"You knew?" asked Ashling, sitting straight up. "You knew, and you didn't tell me?"

"He asked me not to. He might not go, we don't even know if he'll get the grades."

"Matt gets everything he wants. I bet those A*s will be flying into his exam results."

"You're being unfair, Ashling," said Sketch. On the issue of university, she was stuck in the middle of the two, but if she were truthful with herself she didn't want him to go either. Matt featured heavily in her routine and she'd already lost Maud. Her friendship with Maud had been cut short when the older woman died in a road traffic accident with a bus on Kentish Town Road. Even knowing her friend's energy had moved on and was now a different form didn't remove the sense of loss Sketch experienced. The thought of losing another person she loved frightened her. However, she also knew going away to continue his education was important to Matt and tried to balance it against him having a responsibility to be there for his son, Sammy. As if on cue, Clock, the old furry cat Maud had left behind when she died, sidled up and rubbed herself against Sketch's legs. Sketch bent forward to stroke her.

"Now, you're taking Matt's side? I thought you were my friend," said Ashling. The conversation had spiralled into negativity, and Sketch struggled to do anything to lighten things. It all brought back the times she'd failed to make things work in the Core, resulting in terrible things like the computer crashing.

"Sorry, it's not like that. We talk sometimes."

"You talk? I've seen you twice since you started the gardening course. I thought you were busy with your new friends, but it's obvious you've been spending time with Matt."

Sketch fidgeted, biting her lip before continuing. "What's wrong with that?"

Ashling looked like a volcano inside her was poised to erupt. Sketch thought about hiding behind a cushion but instead attempted a weak smile.

"You don't get it, do you? You don't get any of it. We keep your secret, support you, help you to be like us, but you'll never be a human. Leave us alone." She pulled Sammy towards her, turning away from Sketch. Sketch crept away, wondering what she'd done wrong and if this was what a wounded animal felt like.

Chapter Thirty-Four

WHEN NOT TEACHING at the college, Clare ran a successful gardening business with her partner. The city, though built up, was home to open spaces, parks, squares and gardens, allowing nature a place amidst the overcrowded manmade environment. They had started small, with a bicycle and trailer, specialising in managing the back yards and gardens of people who had plenty of money but lacked the time to dig in and keep things growing as they should. Their company, Urban Rootz, tackled jobs as small as watering outdoor container plants while people flew off on holidays to warmer or colder climes, to landscaping larger gardens and working on community allotment projects. Clare enjoyed the variety, but she gained the most satisfaction from her teaching at the college. Inspiring young minds to consider the natural world and grow things in the city seemed the perfect way to pass on her skills to the next generation, not having children of her own. This summer term had added something else to the equation, someone else who might be responsible for changing their lives.

"Is that you love?" A soft male voice came from the back of the workshop, in the space they rented in a small industrial estate in between the Victorian terraces of Kentish Town. She turned to see the man who still made her lips curl upwards into a smile, even after years of many ups and downs. Things weren't always perfect but together they leapt over hurdles and made it to their own personal finish line. Years of living taught her there was always a next race or challenge to be faced but having someone next to you to share it and celebrate the triumphs with made it worth crawling out of bed in the morning; she wasn't a morning person.

"Hello, you," she said. He stood across the room from her, dark skinned and skinny as the proverbial rake. Unlike many men of his age, he'd not ballooned outwards at the stomach as he outgrew his teenage metabolism and somehow retained a youthful appearance, like he was stuck in a physical time warp.

"Did you see her today?" he asked. He wiped his compost covered hands with his dark blue overall. "Do you think it's her?"

She walked across the room, kissed him on the forehead and looked at his face, hope from his eyes beaming into hers.

"Yes, Sketch was there, but Mister, I'm not sure. She's just as you described her, but it's over twenty years later. How can it be possible?"

"But isn't it too strange to be a coincidence?" he asked. "All these years, I've, we've, lived without knowing who I am, where I came from, with only fragments to go on. And now the girl I saw in a vision two decades ago appears in our lives. It has to mean something."

Clare nodded. She wanted there to be something to the Sketch thing. It was remarkable for her to be teaching a girl called Sketch, but her cautious side worried about the effect it would have on Michael if this turned out to be another dead end. In the past ten years, as the Internet grew from a data baby to a fully grown global adult, he dipped in and out of search engines, scouring the web for the mysterious girl who haunted him. Each time he failed to discover anything, his mood sank for days on end. He became dark and withdrawn, and Clare found it impossible to watch. Then, he would settle for weeks, sometimes months, enjoying life with her. Because of this cycle of disappointment, she worried this amazing occurrence would turn out to be nothing more than a cruel coincidence.

'What about if I come to college with you next week? We can say I'm running the session with you. In fact, I could run the session with you."

"I don't know," said Clare. "Maybe we should wait a bit longer."

"Wait for what? For the girl to say something? If I see her it might trigger something. If not, if it turns out to be nothing I'll stop searching, I promise." His big brown eyes pleaded with her, puppy dog sad and excited.

"Well you are my partner," she began.

"Thanks, love. Thanks." He embraced her tightly and she felt, not for the first time, a strange sense of energy emitting from him. His hugs were like nothing she'd ever felt with anyone else. She took it to be love.

Chapter Thirty-Five

DRESSED in what she agreed with Trevor was an appropriate outfit for a meet up which may or may not be a date, Sketch made her way to the cafe deli in the small square where she and Harry arranged to meet. Sketch guessed from the higgledy-piggledy tables and chairs that the tiny space accommodated six to eight people. Behind the counter lived a varied collection of deli products such as fancy sausage, posh pickles, cheese, bags of coffee beans and produce in tins and boxes that looked like it dated from the previous century. The eclectic collection confused her nose with contrasting smells competing for her attention. Sketch preferred a home-grown Lincolnshire pork sausage in her sandwich.

"What can I get you love?" said the man behind the cluttered counter as he fiddled with a pile of papers, stuffing a handful in the pocket of his butcher's apron.

Sketch mused, her eyes looking around the shelves for a clue what was safe to buy. "Could I have a vanilla latte?"

He shook his head. "I'll have none of that sugary rubbish in my coffee. Don't hold by it. Tell you what, you have an espresso." She pulled a face at the thought of drinking a bitter shot of coffee. At least it was short, so it would all be over soon.

"Trust me," said the cafe owner. "If you don't like it, you don't have to pay."

She nodded. As he pressed the coffee down into a metal container and forced water through it, Sketch peered through the door, trying to spy Harry, in part hopeful he would arrive before she tasted the dreaded espresso.

"Here you go." The cafe owner slid a small purple cup in front of her. She examined it, creamy on top but not from milk.

"Do you have any sugar?" she asked.

He pushed the cup further towards her. "Have it without the sweet stuff, trust me."

She raised the cup to her lips and took a sip of the coffee.

"Ummm," she said, taking a second and then a third drink. "It tastes...erm...not bitter."

"It's all about the bean, the water, how much, how hot, how fresh. Glad you like it."

The door to the cafe creaked open allowing a fresh breeze waft in and along with it Harry.

"Hey, Sketch," he said, hands in pocket. "You got a coffee already?"

She nodded. "An espresso. Can I have another one?"

The owner laughed. "Of course, you can, but don't drink too many of them. You'll be bouncing to Timbuktu and back. What would you like?" he turned his attention to Harry.

"Could I have a coke, please mate?"

Sketch steered Harry to the furthest table from the counter, only about a metre away. Even though her new cafe friend had introduced her to espressos, her new favourite drink, she wanted to have a private conversation with Harry. She was intent on learning as much as she could about his life, hoping to unearth a clue to whether or not he had been one of her friends in the Core.

"So," she said.

"So"

She noticed a distinctive twinkle in his eye, the one people use when they are teasing you.

"Nice hair," Harry said.

"You think so?" Harry complimenting her hair caused her to glow. Perhaps this was a date.

"Yeh, it's very, well, it's very you."

The conversation paused. Sketch struggled to think of how to start them talking again.

"How's things?" she asked.

"Things are good."

"Must be weird, moving to London, getting used to everything, making new friends," said Sketch, pausing as the cafe man brought across her second espresso.

"I suppose. It is different here, like London is a different country rather than just city. It's such a huge place, full of stuff to explore. I'm liking learning about it." He took a swig of his coke. "And there's these girls I'm hanging around with, they're alright."

Sketch's eyes looked like they were about to pop out from her head. Who were these girls? He laughed.

"What?" she asked, half confused, and half hurt. "Why are you laughing at me?"

"Because, Sketch, you of the funny name, I'm talking about you and Mae. You are the girls."

"Oh! I thought you meant some other girls."

"Are you jealous, Sketchy?" His twinkle now sparkled, and she began to turn her signature beetroot colour, flushing from the bottom of her neck up to the tip of her head.

"No, why would I be jealous?"

"Ha ha, I'm just messing with you, chicken. But it's good to hear cause I wanted to ask you..."

Sketch's mind was in a whirl of coffee, hot face and the thought that Harry might be going to ask her out on an actual date, and he might want to kiss her. He might want to be her boyfriend. Each thought terrified her and excited her in equal measure. Her final thought stopped all others in their tracks. And what if he was Inco and what if he loved her?

"Sketch?" Said Harry, waving his hands in front of her face and waking her from her thoughts.

"Sorry, sorry." She focused back upon the real Harry rather than the one in her head who could be a million people or things, with endless things he could say. "What were you going to say?"

"It's a bit embarrassing to be honest. Dunno if I should?"

Sketch put on her brightest face and a grin she hoped was appealing and cute.

"You can tell me. I'm understanding. Well Jackie once told me I was getting better at being empathetic."

Harry pulled a face, eyes popping and lips pouting, making her giggle. She watched his features switch to serious mode, distinct from his usual jokey appearance and he was fidgeting with a salt shaker, risking a full flow of its contents into the table.

"It's, well, it's about this girl I like. I'm not sure if she likes me." He flipped his eyes up so they met Sketch's. "How do you know if someone likes you?"

"Oh," said Sketch. This question didn't have an easy answer, at least not one she had access to. Her track record with boys was suspect, her crush on Matt turned out to be unrequited and she lacked the instincts a real human would have when it came to making a romantic match. "Why don't you just ask them?" The words tumbled from her mouth before she could give them a thought.

"What if she doesn't like me?"

I like you, I like you, thought Sketch. "What if she does?" she countered. He smiled at her, relaxing back into his chair.

"Maybe you're right, Sketch."

Chapter Thirty-Six

ON ANY OTHER DAY, Clare looked forward to her sessions at the college. Teaching, it turned out came naturally to her and helped to supplement the Urban Rootz's income, especially during the winter months when bad weather made it harder to make the gardens of London beautiful. The company had a loyal group of clients who paid a retainer in the colder, darker, wetter part of the year, when their plants and flowers required minimum tending. Their custom kept the lights on but jobs like tutoring young people meant they didn't have to worry about eating, socialising and keeping the business afloat. Aside from the money, Clare relished the teaching. Young minds soaked up knowledge, even when they goofed around and feigned disinterest. Growing things from scratch, a seed planted into compost, placed in an incubator and sprouting green signs of life, never failed to inspire moments of awe, and cries of 'wow', and sometimes "it's dope, innit?" or other colloquial expressions of amazement and joy. For many of the students, Gardening 101 was their first experience of looking after something, giving it what it needed to stay alive. It always brought out the optimistic side of them. Today, however, Clare wished she could have stayed in bed.

A colony of cold germs were using her body as their headquarters, making her snotty, fussy and victim of a heavy headache.

"Thanks, you," she said through the mucus collecting in her nasal cavity, taking the hankie offered up to her and blowing a mountain of snot into it. "Yuck."

"Are you sure you don't want to give it a miss today? I can run the class for myself."

The offer was well meant, and she knew he had memorised the lesson plan, but this was her class, her responsibility. The other reason nerves were battling with cold symptoms for control of her head, was because her lovely other half planned to be there observing the session. She didn't know how he would react, how it would be when he saw Sketch and finally came face to face with the girl with the unusual name. What if it wasn't her? And what if it was? Could it be possible that their lives linked in some way? It would all be so much easier to think about if her nose wasn't blocked and her throat not as scratchy as hell.

"It's alright. Just come and watch, talk about the business at the end like we planned. They're a nice bunch this lot."

"Okay, I'll just pop out the back and get us a tea from the thermos," he said. "It might help your throat."

Clare wished that were true but became distracted by the telltale prodding itch of an oncoming sneeze. As the collected germs projected themselves with an accompanying "Atchooo" the first of her students appeared in the classroom and began staking claim to tables.

"Bless you, Miss," said Dwayne as he pulled out notebooks, pens and his smartphone.

"Thanks, Dwayne. Hello, everyone. As you can probably guess, I'm a little poorly but there's nothing strenuous planned for today. We'll be examining different types of compost and their uses, and as an extra, not on the syllabus, item, we've got a guest."

"Who's that then? The invisible man?" Harry laughed as he gazed around the room, his hands cupped around his eyes to impersonate binoculars. Both Sketch and Mae looked up at him, with worshipful smiles. *Oh, the class clown, I could do without the funnies today,* thought Clare. She considered a stern face but realised it would only make him try to be funnier to impress the girls, or maybe the boys.

"He's my business partner. He's making tea, and before you ask, he's making me a cuppa, not you." Her eyes met Harry's as his mouth started to open to reply and then clamped shut, his head giving the smallest of nods.

"You might not know this but when I'm not here talking to you about nurturing nature, I run a company called Urban Rootz. We thought it would be interesting for you all to hear what you can do outside of your own gardens, window boxes or kitchen sink-side herbs. Ah, here he is. Meet Michael."

Through the door to the college garden area and its greenhouse and compost heaps, came Michael with two mugs of tea and a packet of heavy duty throat lozenges between his teeth. He scrambled for a place to put the hot mugs and the medicinal sweets fell from his mouth onto the lino covered floor as he tried to speak. Sniggers came from the usual suspects, who had their phones set to video anything they could share on social media.

"Hello, everyone," he managed to say, dropping the packet of lozenges to the desk. Clare saw his eyes dart around the room, from student to student, their primary mission to identify Sketch from the jumbled classroom line up. "I'm Michael, the other half of Urban Rootz. Clare's invited me in today. As she's not feeling one hundred percent, perhaps you can all introduce yourselves. Just your name is fine. I know you do the what's the favourite flower/plant thing in the initial session."

He perched on the desk, his fingers gripping the edge, the only thing giving away his concentration and nervousness. Clare knew him well enough to spot the giveaways. She realised Michael hadn't recognised Sketch just from scanning the room, that no immediate glimpses had triggered a clue or vision despite Sketch being the only tall, blonde girl in the group. Perhaps it was all just a coincidence.

Sketch grinned at them both. "I'm Sketch, it's fantastic you can join us. I love learning new stuff, but everyone thinks that makes me weird."

Michael recoiled, knocking over first one mug and then another, in a mini domino effect. His face blanched and he turned to face Clare. She tried to catch him as he sank to the floor into a pool of warm tea stained water, but her hands only caught the edges of his shirt.

Chapter Thirty-Seven

A HALLMARK of a modern librarian was the ability to turn your hand to any sort of challenge, from managing the stock and finding new and exciting ways to display books so they appealed to a range of audiences, to dealing with the occasional bolshie member of the public and the never-ending pile of paperwork. Fortunately, Begw excelled in admin, taking a pragmatic, organised approach to the things she could do and delegating the more tiresome tasks to Trevor. This was in part a natural habit, but she attributed much of her administrative talents to a 1960s guide to being the perfect secretary someone had given her as a joke one Christmas way back in her student days. It turned out to be one of the best presents she ever received. Had it been written it Welsh she would have placed it at the top of the list.

Although book returns sat piled up on the trolleys by the returns desk, waiting to be returned to the shelves, she chose to ignore them, instead picking up a pile of post from the in-tray hidden behind the counter and retired to the staffroom with her council issued laptop. Cup of coffee in hand, she sliced open each of the envelopes before emptying them of their content. The majority of communications now arrived by email or via the council messaging system, and most finances were sent to the finance department at the town hall. Because of its scarcity, opening the mail ranked at the top of Begw's daily tasks. She flipped open the first letter.

"Oh."

Begw reviewed its contents before discarding it and checking the pages from the other white envelopes. Using her favourite pen, the one which made the green ink skate across the page, she scribbled notes on each of the letters, blew on them to check they were dry and shovelled the pages into a paper folder marked *Begw's documents - Keep Out.* She made a second cup of coffee, activated her phone's screen and selected *Winston O, destroyer of dreams* from her contact list.

"Hello. Put him on the phone, please," she said into the faceless microphone. "I don't care if he's entertaining the Pope or the President of the USA, I want to speak to him now." She listened, her face set firm without a hint of a smile. Trevor came in from the public area singing something sounding like Nah, nah, nah. She shushed him, she couldn't stand Kylie songs.

"Yes, I understand. Tell him I called, Marilyn." She hung up the call and grabbed her bag and emergency umbrella. No rain featured in the forecast but then today wasn't going to plan.

"What's going on?" asked Trevor.

"Can't tell you, not yet. And don't look at me like that. I know you don't like not being in on the secret, but believe me, be grateful you're not." Trevor raised one eyebrow after the other, a signature facial expression he was trying to perfect.

"If you say so. Suppose I'd best grab a panad and get back out there then," he said, with a nod towards the library floor. Begw attempted a smile but it didn't make it to her mouth.

"See you later."

Trevor lifted the kettle and judging it had enough water in it flipped it on to boil. As he twisted back around to look for a clean mug a piece of paper lying on the floor, not far from the door, caught his eye.

"Maybe it's a memo," he said to himself and laughed. Begw was a big fan of the memo, a long since dated means of workplace communication before computers introduced email and messaging.

As the water in the kettle whirred and hissed, he picked it up and scanned the contents. Recognising it as a copy of a personal email, Trevor considered putting it back where he found it, or folding it up and leaving it in Begw's in-tray, but he loved a story and this story appeared to be about love. His nosy nature got the better of him and he slunk down into the green office comfy chairs and began to read the email.

If it was a film, thought Trevor, then key words would jump out in bold and funky fonts on the screen. The words and phrases would be miss you, outdoor life, great job, and Australia. Australia! The email was from Begw to some woman called Deborah who from the tone of her words was an old flame. And the gist of it was Begw planned to a pack up her life, abandon them and move to the other side of the world. No wonder she'd been acting odd. Trevor wished he could unread the email. Sometimes it was better not to know, but he couldn't forget the words on the page. They were like when an image seems burnt onto your retina, no matter how much you blink or close your eyes, it's still there. He folded the paper back and placed it on the floor where he'd found it, unsure whether or not to confront Begw. He couldn't believe that she would sell them out for a redundancy package, but the email suggested otherwise.

Chapter Thirty-Eight

AFTER THE STRANGE day at college, Sketch felt out of sorts. Someone collapsing in front of you brought home the fragility of human life and memories of her friend Maud and her untimely death. She still missed Maud but even her happiest memories of the old woman failed to banish her melancholic mood. Matt and Ashling were still ignoring her messages, and when she popped by the library Trevor acted uninterested in her worries. She was alone in this world, out of place, lost with no way home. The hardest thing was knowing no one could understand what her other life had been like.

Instead of going back to the flat, she found her feet taking her to Jackie, Matt and Ashling's house. If she was going to have a pity party she might as well have it in comforting surroundings.

"Hello," she called out as she walked into the hall. Sounds of the radio playing drifted up from the downstairs rooms, something from the eighties which she knew enough from the data download received before leaving the Core to hum along with.

Reaching the bottom of the stairs, she poked her head into the kitchen and looked around for signs of human life. The sight of

Jackie, dancing on her own in the small galley kitchen caused her to laugh. Dancing brought joy to all those doing it but after the age of twenty-five adult jigging began to look odd.

"Sketch!" exclaimed Jackie. She stopped in her tracks, paused for a moment before starting to dance again. "Come on, join me." Jackie held out her hand to Sketch, so she took it and began to swizzle, turn and move to the beat, letting the vibrations of the music move her.

"Enough!" said Jackie, struggling to catch her breath as the song came to an end and the voice of the DJ took over.

"Are you okay?"

"Just getting old."

"I'll make you a cuppa. You just sit down, and I'll bring it over," said Sketch. She grinned at Jackie, still fuelled by the power of dancing and wanting to do something nice for the woman who was for all intents and purposes her human mother.

"I wouldn't say no. So, what's all this about you, Ashling and Matt fighting?"

Sketch popped a couple of tea bags into a pretty green teapot the perfect size for two. "Oh, Jackie. I've really messed up. Neither of them wants to speak to me. Thing is, I thought it would help." She paused. "I don't think I'm cut out to be a human. I mess up everything." She carried a tray with the pot, milk, cups and biscuits through to living room, placing it down on a side table Jackie dragged in front of the sofa.

"Come here, hon. I think what you need is a hug." Jackie enfolded her arms around Sketch and held her there. Sketch remembered the power of human touch, the energy it brought to a situation, its warmth, and she managed a small smile as the two bodies pulled away from each other.

"What you are feeling is as human as it gets, especially at your age. I wouldn't be your age again for all the tea in China."

"What about all the sausages in London?"

Jackie laughed. "No, not even for all the prosecco in Tufnell Park. It's a painful age. You're all finding out who you are and where you fit in the world. And don't you start imagining you make a mess of everything. We all love you."

"Do you really? Don't you have to love me because I'm stuck here?"

"Oh Sketch, we love you for so much more. We're privileged you're still here with us, although of course we want you to be able to go back." Jackie leaned across and took Sketch's hand. "And don't you worry about Ashling and Matt. They're driving me mad, but their argument's not with you, their gripe is with each other."

Sketch squeezed Jackie's hand, took a deep breath and attempted another cheery smile.

"But neither of them is replying to me. What should I do?"

"Sometimes it's better to get old school about it." Sketch gave her a quizzical look. "It just means do it the old way," said Jackie.

"Write a letter and put it in the post with a stamp?" Sketch guessed her answer was wrong when Jackie gave a little chortle. "No? What then?"

"Talk to them. Just sit down like we are now, with a cup of tea, or a glass of wine and have a chat. I think it will help them too. Why don't you stay for dinner?"

"What is it?"

Sketch was mortified as Jackie looked back at her wide-mouthed. "It doesn't matter what it is. I'll eat it anyway." She clamped her hand over her mouth and then removed it quickly, keen to undo any offence her words might have given. "What I mean is, I love all your food."

Jackie's earlier chortle grew into a full blown deep bellied laugh. "I'm just kidding. I'm making bangers and mash. Almost as if I knew you were coming isn't it?"

Sketch grinned. Somehow, she felt one-hundred percent better than when she'd walked in through the front door. "Will Ashling and Matt be here?"

"No, tonight it'll just be us. Ashling is off with Dominic and Matt's at his dad's.

"Bangers and mash it is then."

"Now then," said Jackie. "I want an update on you and this boyfriend of yours, Harry? When do I get to meet him?"

The red blood flow of blush roused itself on Sketch's face.

"He's not my boyfriend. At least I don't think so." Jackie raised her left eyebrow. "I think he might be from the Core."

Chapter Thirty-Nine

MICHAEL'S MIND raced through cycles of disbelief, relief and terror. His collapse in the college in front of students created a minor panic, bringing first aiders with accident reports to be signed off and students peering through the door attempting to share the moment by photo and video with the world at large via the Internet. After years of wondering and psychiatric treatment, with clues leading to tall brick walls of nothingness, he had an answer, he knew the truth, a truth nobody would ever believe.

Clare brought over a glass of water and a packet of the choco-late chip cookies from the corner shop he loved almost more than her. She sat next to him, her knees pulled to her chest, holding them in place with the protective cage of her arms.

"If it's something bad you can tell me. Have you ever known me to judge? Well, maybe a little about Rebecca, but you were young then. Whatever it is, it happened almost a lifetime ago." He turned his head to look her in the eyes. If he'd had any doubts about her honesty, her face told him he was safe to speak, but a giant jugger-naut of knowledge had rammed into him, catching him up with everything he'd ever been or done and it didn't match up with the life he now led.

"I'm not sure where to start. You'll want to call for the men in white coats to take me away."

"You know me better than that. The girl in your vision has always been at the root of the mystery, so was it Sketch? Start with Sketch." He took a gulp of water, inhaled a biscuit for its sugar content to steady his physical symptoms, and took a deep breath.

"Sketch triggered my memories. When they came back to me they didn't trickle through in fits and starts and jigsaw pieces. They arrived in a torrent of data, too much for my human body to cope with."

"That's why you fainted?"

He nodded. "Like when you overload the washing machine or give a plant too much water after a dry spell. I'm still shaky now." He took another cookie and nibbled at it.

"So, who is she? How do you know her?"

"Sketch is, was, my best friend; my closest companion." He bit his lower lip, took her hand. "It was a long time ago, but I think I loved her." He knew Clare well enough to know that his words would hurt and that she would hide any tears fighting to escape from her eyes. She was only human after all. He on the other hand was anything but.

"What I'm going to tell you requires you to believe in things your education hasn't taught you, to believe in a science that goes beyond current knowledge and understanding."

"I'll try Mister, I promise."

He breathed, closed his eyes then flicked them open to take in her face, inhale her smell, hear her movement and search for her aura.

"Sketch comes from another world, we both come from another world. Not a world so much as what you might think of as a dimension."

Clare opened her mouth but closed it again.

"Best not to ask questions yet. Listen to everything I'm going to tell you then fill the room with them, with your doubts and disbelief. I only hope you leave space for a kernel of understanding to grow inside you." Clare nodded, and Michael mirrored her gesture. "The world, the universe is made up of elements. Your science knows about the periodic table, teaches it at schools in physics lessons to kids full of hormones, who are navigating the world via their phones. You also teach them about energy, but the extent of your knowledge only skims the surface. The truth is everything is made up of energies. They are the base components of the universe and beyond."

Clare's lips moved silently forming the word beyond. Michael realised his words were beginning to bounce off her brain and he would have to skip to the point soon, before the limits of her mind resulted in it shutting down.

"Energies transform from one thing to another, a little like reincarnation. Of all your religions the Buddhists are closest to the truth."

Shaking herself, Clare sat up straight. "So, we're all energies and we were something else before like a pony or a tree?"

"Yes, those things but also others, like a computer or a television. Millions of energies make those things work. Before I transformed into a human, into this cumbersome flesh being, I performed the function of a computer energy."

Clare laughed. "Oh, that's good. That's so good, you almost look like you're telling the truth. How are you keeping a straight face?"

Michael noticed Clare's body was shaking and her laughter become shrill as his face remained fixed in serious mode. He gauged, through years of time spent getting to know his wife, that her laughter was without humour. And there was nothing funny about the situation they found themselves in. Him, conflicted by his human experience and the loss of his world in the Core, and Clare because she knew something was wrong. Either Michael's mental health had taken a dramatic tumble, or he was telling the truth. Neither option came chocolate-coated.

Chapter Forty

SKETCH EXAMINED Jackie's body language. Head scratching, lips poised ready to speak, shuffling on her seat. All this equalled a negative answer. *Does she think I'm making it up?* thought Sketch.

"You don't believe me, do you?"

"It's not that I don't believe you think he's from the Core, but I'm a little worried," said Jackie, her face softening as she released her words.

"What is there to worry about? If he's from the Core then there will be someone for me to talk to, someone who understands. You try, Matt tries, Trevor does too but none of you have lived my life. It's impossible for you to imagine. You're too, well, you're too human."

"And Harry will get it," said Jackie nodding. "But what concerns me is that the chance of him being one of your fellow energies is so slim."

"But it would make sense if when the Core collapsed, and they activated the emergency protocols, all the energies were transformed to humans."

"They could be anywhere. The world is full of humans, old, young, happy, grumpy, overfed, starving."

Sketch fizzled, she knew she was right. Transformation to this realm would have been easy to effect. It was the last place any of them had transformed to, the location she'd been sent to, so, if the settings were still in place a swift recycling would have been possible.

"If they came here, I could help them. There is a logic to it," she countered, her smile brimming with confidence.

"So, if this Harry is a transformed energy, why hasn't he spoken to you about it?"

Sketch stalled, each time she started to reply she couldn't find words which gave the correct answer. Her human brain prevented her from coming up with a reason why Harry hadn't revealed his true essence.

She snapped at Jackie, "I don't know. But he is from the Core, I'm sure he is."

"Whoa there. I'm trying to help, not to upset you more. Tell you what, it might make a difference if you brought him round. Let us meet him."

A rosy sparkle radiated from Sketch's eyes across her face. You could guarantee Jackie could come up with a practical idea.

"Okay, sounds like an excellent plan. By the way, who is 'us'?" Human thoughts moved from positive to negative without any warning, something which amazed Sketch when it happened to her.

Shoving a biscuit across the table, Jackie smiled which reassured Sketch somewhat.

"It's time we sorted out this business with you, Ashling and Matt."

"Oh, really? They hate me." Sketch slumped back down into her angst. Maybe Jackie didn't understand it after all. Perhaps she'd forgotten what it was like to be seventeen. "I don't think that's a good idea. Forget about it. I'll sort it out myself."

Jackie chuckled. "Nope, you're not getting out of it that easily. It'll be fine. They don't hate you. Sometimes I think you're becoming more like us every day."

Sketch shrugged.

"The teenager in you is strong. Like the force, but with added angst."

"The force?" asked Sketch, taken aback by the random physics reference.

"Not that human then," said Jackie grinning. "It was a reference to 'Star Wars', a famous science fiction film. Must have escaped your data download."

"Oh. I think the data is corrupting itself. The download is linked to the Core and if it's no longer there it won't be maintained or updated."

"That explains it then. Well, we've still got the Internet and a vast array of human experience to share with you while you are here."

She thought about Jackie's idea. It might not be such a bad thing for the others to meet Harry. Then they'd see she was right. Rising from her seat she grasped Jackie within her arms and bombarded her with a giant, all-encompassing hug, bringing smiles to both their faces. The power of hugging is something Sketch learned about through both online sources and her own experience. The optimum time for embracing another was between three and five seconds, unless they were your boyfriend or girlfriend in which case a longer hugging period was to be encouraged. The cuddle brought on the feel-good hormone oxytocin and reminded Sketch of a brightening aura as it flooded her body.

"Thank you, Jackie," she said pulling away. "Your excellent plan might well work. Can we do it as soon as possible? And can we have sausages again?"

"Tell you what, you find out when this possible energy boy Harry is free over the weekend and I'll check with Ashling and Matt and we'll fix a date, and I suppose it won't do any harm to have sausages twice in a week."

"Yeh, let's lock it down!" grinned Sketch.

"Lock it down? You sound like you're in some action movie."

"Picked it up from Begw. She says it all the time."

Spending time with Jackie lightened Sketch, lifted some of the anxiety about Harry from her mind. As she gathered her belongings and gave Jackie another, briefer hug, her thoughts turned to messaging him about the visit. For once, things felt like they were falling into place. She'd text him now and then go home and crack on with her gardening course homework.

- Hey Harry. I've been invited to tea with some friends at the weekend. Would love you to come with me. There'll even be sausages. Do you like sausages? I bet you do. Everyone loves sausages.

She read the text back, wondering if she should erase the bit about sausages but Harry was bound to share her passion for the pork filled goodies. She pressed send and kissed her phone for luck before popping it into her bag.

"Bye, Jackie," she shouted as she bounced up the stairs and into the warm air of the London night

Chapter Forty-One

THE LIBRARY WAS CLOSED on a Sunday but because of his employment Trevor had keys he could use and the alarm pin to open the back door. Letting a group of locals in by the public entrance was too risky so one by one they traipsed by the wheelie bins and random cats hanging out in the alley leading to the back of the building. The older members of the group pretended to be undercover agents looking furtively over their shoulders and appearing more conspicuous than the average TV spy. Their move-ments provoked stifled giggles and eye rolling from their younger counterparts. The group was composed of ten of the library's supporters from the local community who had spearheaded the campaign to prevent its closure.

Once collected into the nether regions of the self-help section, Trevor called the group to attention. They continued to talk and shuffle, giggle and gossip with one another including the obligatory exchanges about how hot it was and how life would be much more tolerable once it started to rain again. Not keen on being ignored, Trevor dragged a chair in front of him and stood on it. Sometimes the sight of a person doing something peculiar like standing on a chair in a closed library in semi-darkness caused people to pay attention. With luck, this was one of those times.

"Hello everyone. It's a bit difficult to see in here so try not to bash into the books or the health and safety police will be after me," said Trevor. His face though deadpan, twinkled.

"You'd best come down off the chair then," said Mrs Harding-Edgar. A smattering of laughter spread across the group as Trevor lowered himself back to the vinyl floor.

"There's been a development in the library closure situation. One I thought I should update you about." His audience now focused their attention on his words, except Mr Barrington, who waved his phone about in the air.

"Yes, Mr Barrington," said Trevor, keen to get any further distractions out of the way.

"How do I take a picture?" asked the silver-haired man. Trevor sighed inwardly but shook himself. It wasn't Mr Barrington's fault he struggled. Trevor suspected he was in the early stages of dementia. After promising to show him later, he asked everyone else not to post anything online about today's gathering.

"Right now, I'm sharing things I'm not supposed to be privy to. However, it's not something I believe I can keep to myself." He cleared his throat. "This week, I've seen evidence the library is to be shut down in three months' time."

"But what about the public consultation? They can't just rail-road the will of the people," said Flo Foster.

"Yeh, what about the public consultation?" demanded Dominic's sister Rochelle, who'd been involved with the campaign since the beginning. Voices muttered, and heads nodded in agreement.

Trevor held his hands up in a waving down gesture. "If you hang on for a minute I'll finish." Begw and Sketch were so much better at this rousing the crowd stuff, it was like leading story time with giant children. But he couldn't rely on Begw now he knew she was planning to jump ship. And with Sketch struggling to adjust to being stuck in the human world and all that meant for her, he didn't want to burden her with the weight of this enormous problem.

"The document I read mentioned the public consultation but

said the evidence wasn't strong enough to prevent shutting down the library. The powers that be have legal advice which backs it up. The injunction over the lack of consultation was the only thing holding them back. With that out of the way, they can go ahead with their plan.

"But there must be something we can do." said Mrs Harding-Edgar. Trevor noticed tears welling in her eyes and couldn't stop himself from putting his arms around her for a hug while he accepted a paper tissue from Mr Barrington, who always seemed to be prepared for tears.

"Not much. I've been in touch with some other services who've been down this road and they seem to think we've come face to face with a sink hole." Faces dropped around him. "They did give me one suggestion but it's a long shot."

"What? Tell us then laddie. Don't keep it all to yourself."

"There's a chance we can take it on and run it on a voluntary basis, but we need funding and support."

"What? You mean we'd run it? But we don't know anything about running a library. We're not librarians."

"But Trevor and Begw are. They could help, eh Trevor?"

He pondered what to reply. Despite being hurt and angry at Begw's betrayal he didn't think it right to out her behaviour to this lovely group of people who adored her.

"I'll do what I can, but both of us will need to find other jobs too."

"They won't redeploy you then?"

"Nowhere to deploy us to. We're not the only location earmarked for closure."

The room fell silent. Trevor looked from face to face wondering how to break this awkward deadlock.

"We'll just have to leap across that bridge when it happens, but I'll do everything I possibly can short of jumping in front of a bus."

Faces brightened a little as if given a reassuring hug or some chocolate cake. Trevor remained worried but tried hard to stop it showing on his expression. He feared the positive effects of virtual cake and promises of help wouldn't last long. What he planned to do would take considerable time, tenacity and a love of the library. Looking around he realised he'd assembled a rescue squad who had all these attributes and he wasn't going to allow the council, Begw and their dastardly plans to take away the library, a vital resource for the local community. They were all people in suits making short-term decisions with no thought to how it would affect real people living in the area.

"Right, let's crack on with it. We've a lot of planning and plotting to do."

From the left of the gathering of locals, behind a bookcase, Begw slipped away shaken by what she'd heard and at a loss to know why Trevor hadn't invited her.

Chapter Forty-Two

WHEN FACED WITH THE IMPOSSIBLE, difficult, or unfathomable, Clare did what she always had since moving to London and headed out to Hampstead Heath, one of the green spaces within the sprawling urban density of London where you could connect with nature. The Heath, like the marshes and wetlands of Tottenham, Hackney and Walthamstow, gave people a chance to escape from human designed landscapes of concrete and sculptured parks in favour of a wilder environment with a diversity of animal and plant species. Fungi grew, birds tweeted in chorus and grasses, weeds and flowers coexisted without the judgement of humans as to what belongs where. The land was cultivated but, in a manner which preserved the way of nature.

Clare stomped up Parliament Hill with the intention of getting to the least populated and most natural area of the Heath. The swimming ponds fulfilled this function, but she wasn't one for water sports, having swallowed too many mouthfuls of water and snorted too many of them out of her nose as she flapped around trying to swim and look coordinated at the same time. Instead, she headed for a copse of trees by her favourite clearing.

Along the way she turned to take in London, a view she found inspiring. But Michael's revelation had shaken her, and she couldn't focus on the beauty of the cityscape. If what he told her was true, and she was in no doubt he believed it to be, then what did it mean for her understanding of reality? Everything she thought she knew disintegrated. The buildings in front of her eyes, the cars populating the congested roads of the city, the phones people held in their hands and everything growing around her. She sighed. Perhaps there was a sound reason humans didn't know such things. *I'm not evolved for this,* she thought.

Reaching her favourite space, Clare pulled a waterproof blanket from her tote bag and spread it onto the uneven grassy ground. She found a comfortable position and slid down on her back, giving her eyes a perfect view of the cloud splattered sky above, framed by a ragged circle of leaf covered tree branches.

"What should I do?" She asked to no one in particular. She didn't have a god, a faith or a priest to share with or pray to. All she had was her belief in science and the miracle of nature. No answer came from the sky, but her mind felt soothed by its vastness. No matter what drama crashed into their lives the swirls of the atmosphere and the whims of the weather continued regardless.

One of the options she considered was convincing Michael to talk through his convictions with his former psychiatrist, but this would be doing him a disservice if it turned out to be true. But how could it be? How could he be someone who came from inside a hard drive? Maybe she was the one who needed help with her mental health. Her mother had been a mental health professional and could have helped, but she had died years ago of a stroke. Clare bolted upright. Did that mean her mum was now something else? Like reincarnation, 'cos after all that's sort of what Michael believed had happened to him. Transformation, recycling, reincarnation; they could all be one and the same.

She closed her eyes and inhaled, practising the regulated breathing picked up at her yoga class.

"Hey there."

Flipping her eyes open and shielding them from a random ray of sun, Clare stared towards the familiar voice. She recognised the features of the woman in front of her but failed to match them to a name.

"Sorry if I'm disturbing you. I'm Jackie, Sketch's guardian. We met the other week when Sketch brought me in to look at her Kale."

There seemed to be no way for Clare to escape away from Sketch. If she believed in such things she might think the universe was sending her signals, but plenty of scientific studies showed coincidences happened by random chance.

"Oh of course. Hello. Sorry, I was miles away. It's so peaceful up here."

"That's why I come up here. The world sometimes gets a lot of crazy," said Jackie. "Especially with a load of teenagers struggling with where they fit in the world and with each other."

"If only that stopped when you became an adult," said Clare with a sigh.

"Look I don't want to intrude but I've got a freshly brewed flask of chamomile, honey and vanilla tea here if you fancy a cuppa?"

Clare felt a rush of affection towards the hippy looking woman in front of her. "You know what? Tea's exactly what I need. Come and join me." She patted the blanket, shifting her bag out of the way to make room for Jackie.

"So, teenager problems, is it?"

"One who's a single dad at seventeen and wants to go to university, the other the mother of my gorgeous grandchild Sammy who also wants to go to uni. We've no money for either of them to go really."

"What about Sketch? Is that what she wants to do too?"

Jackie rolled her eyes. "Sketch is a joy but even more complicated than the two human ones."

"What?"

"Oh sorry, just on the whole she's full of positivity unlike your average teen but she's not got her family around her which is hard. Oh!" Jackie clamped her hand over her mouth. "That was a terrible thing to say about teenagers. And I do love my Matt and Ashling."

"It's a delightful age to be. All that possibility, everything ahead, but it's a lot for them." Clare turned the plastic cup of tea around in her hands.

"Sorry, I'm hogging this." She passed it across to Jackie.

"Are you okay?" asked Jackie. "Here I am rambling on about my lot and their angst."

"Not really. Someone and by someone, I mean my partner Michael..."

"The one who collapsed this week? Sketch mentioned it."

"Yes, that's him. He's okay. Sort of. He just told me something unbelievable."

"Really? If you want to share I promise it won't go any further. You wouldn't believe the unbelievable things I know."

"It all sounds crazy, even to me. But here goes."

Chapter Forty-Three

AFTER DAYS of what felt like unending sunshine had transformed London into a happy place of people wearing skimpier than usual clothing without anyone for the most part blinking an eye, the weather shifted back to dull grey with persistent drizzle. Begw examined her hair in the lift mirror. Ten minutes of blow drying and straightening couldn't compete with the British weather and the result was rogue kinks and curls appearing around her head. She snarled at her expression. Today was going to be difficult enough without her hair betraying her. *Maybe it doesn't drizzle in Australia,* she thought. The lift reached the fourth floor. Its doors slid apart revealing the standard open plan office of civil and public service administration. Although Begw often visited the building for meetings she still found navigating the uniformity of rows of desks, now hot desks used by whoever claimed them each day, challenging. What she did remember was that Winston's office sat in a corner on the fourth floor and she would reach it by eliminating the other corners as she went.

She nodded at Marilyn, Winston's assistant, knocked and pushed open the door to his office without waiting for an invitation.

"Well, well, well," he said, sitting back on his chair, spreading his arms and legs as far as they could go. "If it isn't Little Ms Let's Save the Library."

"Quit with the patronising, mock surprise. We had an appointment."

He stared at her, bloodshot eyes bulging. She stared back. Although it was tempting to engage in a full-on staring contest like a pair of kids, Begw was here for another, more pressing purpose. She put on her best game face, sat down in the empty chair by his desk and presented him with a thin beige manila folder.

Winston dragged it across the desk and flipped it open.

"Is it signed?"

"No, not yet. I want some assurances."

Winston rolled his eyes. "You people are always wanting this and that. Why make it complicated? I've got you a good deal, haven't I?"

"A good deal! A good deal would be not closing the library, putting us all out of a job and depriving local people of essential services." Winston opened his mouth to reply but Begw continued, in full flow. "What you're offering is a pay-out, silence money. The only reason I'm giving it a second thought is to try to give it a digni-fied ending."

"So, what is it you want other than the overly generous redun-dancy package?"

She scowled the type of scowl you feel inside but hide from your face and considered each word before it left her mouth.

"I want you to think about letting someone else take over the library."

Winston rolled his eyes and sniggered. Begw expected nothing less. He was an odious man whose incompetence would end up getting him promoted or employed in a higher managerial position in another borough.

"People don't take over failing services. There's no money in it. Besides which the council need the building. It's an important asset."

"What exactly do you mean by important asset?"

Winston stared at her. It was as if he had the attention span of a goldfish and she realised it was unlikely he would tell her the truth, although she'd already guessed what it was.

"By important asset, do you mean selling it to a big developer who only intends to build swanky flats for rich people?"

"I have no idea what you're talking about. How would I know what the council's property team plans to do? I'm Head of Library Services not the planning department. Unless there is something constructive you wish to say I suggest now is a good time to leave." He stood up and gestured towards the office door. Begw sighed. This was going to be harder than she first imagined. There was another card to play, but now might not be the ideal moment. Despite this, she didn't want Winston to have the upper hand. She chewed it over, realising the best thing to do might well be to keep quiet for now. She rose from the chair.

"My mother always told me if I didn't have something nice to say not to say anything at all. "She left the room without a further word in Winston's direction. Before leaving the building, she stopped to have a few words with his secretary. There was information to be collected and evidence to be collated before she put her final plan in play.

On exiting the building, she checked her phone messages and emails. Nothing popped into her inbox from Australia. She felt an instant sense of disappointment. A reply of some sort might give her some peace of mind, a sense she was making the right decision, not just for herself and her heart, but for those she cared about. Instead there was nothing, nothing but a sense of emptiness and a building anxiety.

Chapter Forty-Four

ON A BENCH in the corner of the college courtyard sat Sketch and Mae. By their sides were triple-choc salted caramel lattes with extra ice and Sketch munched a home-made sausage sandwich. Now that she lived with Trevor, Sketch was aware that buying a sausage sandwich and a triple-choc salted caramel latte each day was well beyond her budget. With the help of Trevor's culinary skills, which were generally limited, she learned how to make her own sandwiches. While not the same as going to Greggs or the college canteen - the sausages were cold by the time she got around to eating them - it gave her a level of satisfaction to learn a new skill. That was the amazing thing about living in the human world, there was always something new to learn. In fact, she thought she would never stop learning.

"So, he's coming for dinner at your house?" asked Mae.

Sketch shook her head. "Not exactly. He's coming to Jackie's house. She wants to meet him."

"And Jackie?" Said Mae battling with a chocolate chip cookie. "She's like your mum?"

Sketch nodded. "The closest thing I have to a mum, being so far from home."

"Is your mum like dead then?"

Mae's question was a difficult one for Sketch to answer without going into the truth. Telling Mae where she came from, that she was not from this world, could be risky. She didn't want her friends to think she was weird or unusual, even if she did have rainbow coloured hair.

"No, she's not dead. She is a long way from here and I miss her in ways I never expected."

"You're homesick, innit? That's what it is. Good job you got this Jackie." Mae put her drink to the side, leaned in and gave Sketch a massive hug which made the energy smile. Mae was the giver of hugs. She told Sketch it was the same with her family, all of them partial to an all-embracing cuddle. "And you've got me, which I know isn't the same, but I am kind of cool."

Having friends made everything easier. It reminded Sketch of the cliché about a trouble shared being a trouble halved. While she doubted the mathematical accuracy of the phrase, the sentiment rang true for her. She grinned at Mae.

"Big head!"

"But you know it's true. You knows it. Now, back to the important stuff."

"Harry?"

"Yes, Harry. Is it lurrrrve?"

"No, but he's cute and he's got a cool accent being from the North."

"His voice isn't the only thing about him that's attractive," said Mae, giggling and nudging Sketch. "Know what I mean?"

Before Sketch could reply, the tall, solid figure that was Harry whisked away the remains of her sausage sarnie, leaving her in the unusual predicament of being without words and unsure whether or not she cared. She adored sausages and had been known to get ninja over their theft, but Harry stealing it from her made it somehow different. Perhaps he needed the sarnie more than her. Maybe all former computer energies fixated on the delicious fatty taste of the sausage.

"Oi! Give it back to Sketch."

Harry popped the remains of the stolen lunch into his mouth, still managing to give them a cheeky, 'try and make me' type grin.

"It doesn't matter," said Sketch. "I'm full and it's hard to resist the allure of a good sausage." Mae's eyebrows rose higher than Sketch thought possible.

"Sketch. Harry is a boy, a boy thief at that. Never, ever put boys before your favourite things. I'm late for intro to hairdressing." Mae picked up her bag, scowled at Harry, winked at Sketch and headed back into the main college building.

Harry parked himself next to Sketch. She smiled at him he smiled back.

"Still on for tonight?" asked Sketch.

"Well, that all depends."

"On what?"

"On whether they'll be more of those delicious sausages for dinner."

Sketch laughed. "I think Jackie is planning to make a lasagne with Italian sausage. Her lasagne is the best ever. And I've not tasted every lasagne ever made so you'll have to take my word for it. But if you don't like lasagne I can ask her to do something else. I know you're not a vegetarian, but do you have any other dietary requirements?"

"Blimey, you speak really fast when you want to. No dietary requirements, lasagne with Italian sausage is cool and as long as you're there I'll be fine."

Sketch felt the hot redness of a blush begin to tomatofy her face. It was one of the few things about being human she didn't like. She had no control over it. Crying was the same but at least with the tears came a sense of relief, blushing just made her appear foolish.

"Thanks," she said. "Come over for seven-thirty and then you'll be able to meet everyone before we eat. As well as Jackie there's Matt her son, and Ashling his ex-girlfriend and their son Sammy will be there too. They're all lovely you're really like them."

"Fine. Oh, Sketch?"

"Yes"

"What's the address?"

Sketch finished finalising the details of the meet up, giving Harry directions to Jackie's house. It occurred to her she didn't know where he lived or anything about his family. Perhaps he didn't have one. This would make sense if you had come from the Core. He was well turned out and clean, so must be living somewhere. She added this to a mental list of things to bring up at dinner. Some of these questions she planned to share with Jackie and get her to do some of the asking. In just a few days' time she would know if Harry was Inco in human form. The thought excited her, bringing back memories of her former life. She was tempted to spiral into a spin and couldn't help wishing she could omit sparks of energy from her aura.

Chapter Forty-Five

JACKIE WAS at a loss as what to do. She couldn't add the dots, not all of them anyway. What Clare told her changed everything. Now the dilemma was what to tell Sketch. Sketch, although still spending time attempting to resurrect the computer, had settled into life in North London and had friends and future prospects. On the other hand, was it fair to hold back this information from her, to give her the chance to connect with someone from her own world, even if the circumstances were tragic?

Over the past few days Jackie and Clare had talked frequently by text, neither sure what best to do. What they could agree on was to let the dinner with Harry go ahead. There was a good chance that during the evening Sketch would realise he was just an average human relocated from the North of England. Plus, the family dinner had been designed to heal the rift between the teens and help Matt and Ashling come to the right decisions about their futures. University, future study, jobs and crucially how they juggled all this with bringing up little Sammy. Jackie found it difficult to relax. Sooner or later she must make a decision about what to tell Sketch. The implications of telling her the truth could shatter everything good Sketch had built up during her time as a human. *Hope*, thought

Jackie *is so very important.* One of the things she most loved about Sketch was the positivity she exuded. Would that disappear when she realised there was no chance of ever returning to the Core?

She moved some finely chopped onions to the side of the chopping board, pulling out some mushrooms ready to prepare for the next steps in the construction of the lasagne. Although Jackie had planned to serve up a healthy vegetarian meal, she decided to throw in the Italian sausages knowing how much Sketch enjoyed them. Whatever came next, this meal was a chance to be a family, to eat together and make decisions together. The following day she would sit down with Sketch and tell her everything, she owed her that at the very least.

There were times Jackie wondered if things wouldn't have been easier if she just ignored those early communications from the One, the head energy in the computer. Or if there was a network of people in the same situation, other human liaisons with this strange unknown world. But it was difficult to know how to go about finding out such a thing. She dropped the knife onto the worktop, her eyes lighting up as an idea started to form and grow and sparkle. Wiping her hands on the nearby tea towel, she scanned the room until she located her phone. As quickly as possible and with the aid of autocorrect she pinged out a message to Clare, reading it out aloud before pressing send.

-Hi, can you ask Michael if he knows about liaisons in the human world? I'll explain later.

Jackie put the phone down next to her, display facing upwards. She stared at it, willing a speedy reply from Clare. Her message looked back at her from the screen, showing no response, no dot dot dot indicating someone was typing. She sighed, feeling anxious. Realising it could be some time before her new friends got back to her, she returned her attention to preparing the evening meal. Something about preparing, chopping, and constructing a dish from scratch with fresh ingredients was soothing and a little creative. Periodically, she glanced back-and-forth at her phone, checking for notifications. She had all but given up when a ping came. Jumping a little, heart racing she unlocked the screen and read a reply, a reply not from Clare.

- Records indicate you are a human, you have been designated status of liaison with a different entity. Your service is no longer required.

Chapter Forty-Six

THE TOWNSEND'S living room sat on the middle floor of the three-storey house. As the family favoured the extended dining room space in the basement, Jackie had transformed the living room into a child-friendly space. Toy boxes replaced nests of coffee tables and the long-haired rugs were moved downstairs to make room for a play mat of a town, perfect for toy buildings, cars and buses and for Sammy to spill his orange squash on without causing any permanent stains or other damage.

Sketch heard the tell-tale sounds of Sammy playing in the living room as she let herself into the house. She arrived earlier than planned so she could talk to Ashling and Matt before Harry joined them for dinner. She tapped on the white panelled door, paused for a second before entering. Sammy had set up a row of dolls and teddies in front of a child-sized whiteboard balanced on a plastic easel. Playing the role of the teacher he instructed them to do PE activities and go to school. On a chair in the corner, Ashling sat with her head buried in a book, jotting notes in a notebook at her side.

"You catching up with homework? asked Sketch. Ashling raised her head up to look across at her friend and nodded. Sketch smiled, only a small smile as she didn't know if Ashling even wanted to speak to her. A sense of relief came over her when she realised Ashling returned her smile. It was a start.

"Got an essay to finish before Monday morning and Dominic is coming over tomorrow."

"Really?" asked Sketch. "It's a shame he couldn't come tonight. We've haven't all hung out for an age."

"I know. He says hi."

"Dom," Sammy piped up before continuing to teach his menagerie of toys. The pair laughed. Sketch never failed be cheered up by the young boy. Something about him reminded her of herself when she first transformed from a computer energy and joined the human world.

"I like him too," Sketch said. "As a friend, not like Matt, oh, I mean Harry."

Ashling's eyes widened lifting her eyebrows extending upwards towards her hairline. "Matt?"

"Slip of the tongue. Matt's a friend too but that's all, nothing more. I meant Harry. He's the one I'm interested in."

"Ummm. Talking of Matt, have you spoken to him lately?"

"No, not sure he wants to see me. I thought you were both mad at me."

"I'm not mad at you, not really. Matt just doesn't think. Sammy has to come first but in the long-term that means me getting a proper education as well as Matt."

Sketch lit up inside. Ashling still wanted to be friends. She jumped over and bombarded her with a giant hug.

"You'll work it out. Remember boys are stupid sometimes. Well, some of them. I can't wait for you to meet Harry. He's not stupid at all."

"Oh, your face is all smiley! Is it love?"

"Well." Sketch paused, thinking through what she knew about the complicated emotion that was love. She went all the way back to her time in the Core, watching Matt and Jackie from other side of the computer screen, viewing their online interactions and shared thoughts, and contrasted it with the science of love and her own experiences as a teenage young woman. She looked back at

Ashling, "It might be romantic love, but I don't know its longevity."

Ashling giggled. "Maybe it's a 'for now' love."

"Where's Matt then?" asked Sketch, remembering she wanted to speak to him too before Harry arrived.

"Up in his room. I'll message him. It's the easiest way to get his attention."

Sketch grinned, but inside she felt squiggly. She hadn't spoken to Matt since the big falling out and had no idea if he even wanted to speak to her. Her insides churned around their contents as if in a human food processor. Despite her nerves, she chuckled to herself thinking that she was indeed processing the food eaten over the last twenty hours.

Ashling put down her phone and beckoned Sketch over for another hug. It made Sketch feel better. Hugs were the equivalents of energies sharing the light, the closest thing she could find to being together with her old friend Inco. But if it turned out Harry was, as she suspected, Inco in human form, it would change everything. As she pulled away from her friend, the door to the living room creaked open and in slouched Matt.

"Hello," he said head down facing the toys on the floor.

"Hello," replied Sketch, her voice just audible across the room. Her eyes dipped up towards Matt's face. Seeing his downward posture, she leapt across the room, avoiding tripping over toy buildings, cars and the odd Lego figure, giving Matt a hug to rival the one she received from Ashling.

"I have missed you," Sketch said continuing to embrace Matt as if both their lives depended upon the ferocity of it.

"Yeh, me too. I mean I missed you, at least a little bit. Not that I missed me." Sketch gave him an extra squeeze as he patted her spiky hair. This was normal, the balance of the universe had fallen back into line, the human universe at least.

"Matt? Ashling?" Sketch looked from one to the other not sure if she should raise the subject of university again. An idea popped into her head as she was walking over from Trevor's flat, but she knew from past experience not all ideas were good ones. It would be awful to upset her friends again. "Don't worry, I'm not sure I should say this."

"It's okay, Sketch. Tell us what it is."

Matt nodded in agreement with Ashling.

Sketch took a deep breath in through her nose and out through her mouth to calm her nerves, like calm together people did on meditation Vlogs. "Can we talk about university? There must be a way to make it work for everyone."

Ashling sighed. "It's not that simple. I wish it was. Matt and I want the same thing but it's not possible for both of us to be at college. Besides childcare, it costs so much money. Do you know how much debt we'll be in at the end?"

Sketch glanced at Matt, his face disappointed but he nodded. "Ash is right. I can't see how we can do it. We have Sammy to think about."

"A year ago, did you think it was possible that your computer was run by energies, or that one of those energies could transform into a human and come and live in your house?" asked Sketch, a glint of light sparkling from her eyes.

"No, but..."

The sound of the front door bell cut Ashling's answer short.

"That must be the infamous Harry," Matt said as Sketch beamed out a grin and sped out of the room.

Chapter Forty-Seven

WITH SKETCH out for dinner with Jackie and her crew, Trevor took the opportunity to crack on with his plan. He opened up his laptop and said hello, a habit picked up from sharing his flat with Sketch. It whirred into action and he picked out the letters on the keyboard which signed him into his video calling account. He still thought it both a blessing and curse to be able to see the person you were talking to through a computer screen. It meant looking your best and putting on your best poker face. So, he changed into one of his favourite shirts and made sure only the tidiest bits of the flat could be seen by the webcam.

The flashing green light indicated @Library_Warrior64was online as planned.

- Hello. Thanks for agreeing to chat.

- Hope I can help. Your email arrived.

- Did you have a chance to read it?

- Yes, so I understand most of the situation. It's not that dissimilar to what we went through, but it would be good to have a bit more detail.

Where should I start?

@Library_Warrior64 glanced down at what Trevor assumed was a piece of paper with a list.

"First off, how much local support do you have? When I say support, I mean do you have enough people with the right skills to be volunteers and run the library?"

"We've got a lot of people and they're really engaged. They led the campaign. But they're a real bunch of characters, some have plenty of time on their hands and others with the skills. I would guess, if I'm being honest, that a small group have both." Trevor thought about his own mental list of the campaigners. Would there be enough people to really do this? Perhaps it was just a pipe dream.

"That's good for a start but you'll need to work up a recruitment strategy, volunteer policies and such. Funders will want to see all that sort of thing has been considered. I can send you a list."

"Thanks," said Trevor. "Do you think I'm, we're mad to do this?"

"Of course."

"Oh."

"You have to be to do this kind of thing," @Library_Warrior64 chuckled. "It will feel impossibly hard. We still struggle now."

"How so?"

@Library_Warrior64 threw up her hands. "What isn't? The hardest thing is people seem to want books less and less. There is the hardcore, those people who can't go a week without changing the books, and fewer people want CDs and DVDs, but we have become a bit of a go to space for people who haven't got anywhere else."

"That's important, especially around here. Can you give me any advice about funding? We can't do this without money."

"Like I said, prepare a proper plan, be clear about what you want and what the outcomes might be. Say what it means for the community and think about what your unique selling point is, what's so special about what you want to do? Why is it so important?"

They continued to chat, Trevor answering @Library_Warrior64's questions and throwing in a number of his own. As they talked he jotted down bullet pointed notes on his phone. By the time the call ended Trevor had collected valuable information on how to go about turning a library service into a volunteer-led community provision. The scale of it was daunting, not least finding the funding to make it happen. The list of funders in front of him provided a starting point but @Library_Warrior64 warned him that many of them had already funded a number of other services across the UK, so would require something new, or packaged up in a different way. And any application should include the word 'innovative' to appeal to those with the purse strings.

Even if they managed to do all this there was still the issue of the building. @Library_Warrior64 suggested they could try to convince the council to rent the space at a peppercorn rent, a token amount. But if that failed? Without the building thousands of books and other resources would be homeless.

Trevor grabbed a nearby cushion from the sofa and threw it across the room groaning out loud. It all seemed impossible. He trudged across the room to pick up the cushion and put it back in its rightful place. Doom and gloom was no excuse for an untidy mess of a living room. The cushion had fallen diagonally across Sketch's computer. Seeing it made Trevor think about his flatmate and her predicament. Sketch was living in an alien world but still managed to stay positive, to have hope, to believe she could fix the computer. *She believes anything is possible,* thought Trevor. He smiled to himself. *If Sketch can be like that then there's no reason I can't be.* He also realised what was missing. By trying to instigate his plan without the spark and enthusiasm Sketch radiated, he was missing a trick. He decided to talk to her as soon as she got back from dinner with the Townsends. In the meantime, he put himself to work sorting through the notes from his call with @Library_Warrior64.

Chapter Forty-Eight

MICHAEL WISHED he could turn back time, travel backwards through the weeks and months of the Gregorian calendar to the day before he remembered the truth about his identity and all the implications which accompanied his revelation. His previous confusion and general sense of being at odds with the world now seemed preferable to knowing for certain he didn't belong, that he couldn't return home, and that the being he loved in his former existence didn't know who he really was. Michael had watched numerous films about aliens, skinny green creatures who were more intelligent, curious and technologically advanced than the planet's native inhabitants. People debated what earth must seem like to an extra-terrestrial being, but Michael had lived it. In his case, however, there was no chance of phoning home, or being rescued by a giant space-craft whose energy usage could run the entire power grid of the Western Hemisphere. He, Michael, former efficient computer energy from the Core, was stuck in this world.

He discussed at length with Clare whether he should contact Sketch, and if he should tell her the truth, but in all their discussions he kept his deepest feelings for Sketch hidden. They were no bigger or better or more than his love for Clare, but his connection with

Sketch centred in his need to belong and an attraction to his own kind.

Clare cautioned against rushing in as Jackie had told her Sketch suspected her boyfriend Harry might be Inco or another energy from her peer group. Telling her that her closest connection wasn't the object of her attraction, but instead a middle-aged man who ran a gardening business with his wife, seemed cruel. Better to keep it to himself and live the life he had. Given his undignified transformation into the human world it was lucky that his life turned out as well as it had. He was fortunate to have met and after some false starts, fallen in love with Clare. And she was beginning to wrap her head around his reality. After her chance meeting with Jackie, Clare began to ask a series of questions, attempting to fill in the gaps in her understanding.

"How did you end up naked in my living room? If the computer broke last year, why did you transform - that's the word right? Like teleporting? Why did you transform into the 1990s? What was it like inside the computer?"

Had the onslaught of questions come from anyone else, Michael would have shrunk from them, but because they came from Clare he tried to answer them the best he could with the limitations of the English language, or indeed all other languages available to him outside the Core.

"When the computer began to fail a plan was put into place to recycle all the energies operating in its space."

"A naked plan?" asked Clare.

"No, but I appreciate your attempt to add some humour into the events. The Core's energies were to transfer to another machine, a newer PC where we could continue our work and use the skills we had to help humans function."

"So, what went wrong?"

"I don't know. If I were to speculate, and using the data available to me, I would say as the functions of the machine became corrupted it defaulted to the last transfer."

"And that was Sketch?"

Michael nodded. "She's the only energy ever to leave the Core in that particular computer. But the timing was wrong, and Sketch was prepared for her transformation. She had a data download to ensure she understood how to behave while living and working with other Londoners. I, we, the other energies that is, had nothing."

Clare topped up their glasses with the remainder of a bottle of red wine.

"We used to observe people and wonder why they drank," said Michael swilling his drink around his mouth appreciating its delicate tones. He thought back to his first few years of living, first in the hostel and later with Rebecca when alcohol cost little and made you feel ill. It gave him little enjoyment it until he went on a wine tasting course. *A wine tasting course*, he thought, *what would Sketch think of that?* She would think it and him boring.

Clare interrupted his train of thought. "What do you mean observe?"

"Two things. We would watch them, mostly Jackie and Matt, through the screen of their monitor. The other way is through the Internet. We read the messages sent by email, social media posts, blogs, news. Everything. What we lacked was an understanding of how it feels to have a body, to have limited understanding of the universe and your place in it. For most of us, that didn't make a difference, but for others, like Sketch, it made it impossible for her to not cause distress to our human users."

"It's like a film. You couldn't make this stuff up if you tried."

"You still think I'm making it up?"

Leaning across the table, Clare grasped his free hand between hers. "Oh lovely, I know you're not making it up, but you have to admit this is a lot to take in."

"It is, and I can't expect you to understand. No one can, no one except..." Michael stopped short of finishing his sentence and appreciated Clare's touch and her understanding smile of reassurance. They sat in the sort of companionable silence which Michael learned came from years of getting to know another person inside out. He felt the warmth of a rush of love for his wife travel through his body. He hadn't chosen this life, but he wanted to stay in it because of the strength of their relationship. Despite this rational thought, his mind began to wander off back to Sketch, his roots and the part of his life he couldn't, wouldn't share with her. *I am Michael,* he reminded himself, *I'm not Inco.*

A dinosaur roar broke the silence. They both stared in the direction of the noise, a mobile phone next to the kettle.

"Do you want me to leave it?" asked Clare.

"No, no you see who it is."

Chapter Forty-Nine

AFTER AN ENLIVENED CHAT with a political campaigner on the doorstep, Sketch and the rest of the family sat around the large kitchen table in the Townsend's basement discussing the merits of distance learning, part-time study and balancing childcare with education.

"Most unis have childcare, crèches and things like that," said Matt. "Sammy could go there during the day."

"You still have to pay for them," said Jackie.

"Oh, I thought they were free for students."

"Some of them are subsidised but on top of fees and clothes and the other bits Sammy needs it's still too much. Neither of us is earning," said Ashling. "And as soon as I become a student I'll lose all my benefits, aside from child benefit."

"So, we work. I get a job now and start saving. What do you think, Sketch?"

Sketch sat straight up at the sound of her name, feeling guilty for tuning out of the conversation.

"Ummm, errrr, sorry. What were you saying?"

Both the large, ticking clock on the wall and her phone read 8:15pm and there was still no sign of Harry, nor had he replied to her messages, emojis and photos of lasagne. Where was he? He could be stuck on the tube on a train held in the tunnel by a red signal. Had he got into a fight with a moving vehicle? Last year, when her friend Maud from the Silver Surfers had died after being struck by a bus, Sketch didn't know for days, instead assuming the older woman was out when she called round to her house. What if something similar had happened to Harry?

"I said I should get a job, save some money for next year to help with childcare while I go to uni and Ashling's finishing her A-levels."

Sketch laughed. She couldn't imagine Matt as a breadwinner. "Great idea but isn't there a lack of jobs around for young people? That's what the perfect looking people on the news keep saying."

Matt shook his head, but Sketch noticed Ashling looked far from convinced as she encouraged Sammy to tuck into his child size portion of lasagne.

"Don't believe everything you see on the telly Sketch. It's like the Internet, full of fake news. There's sure to be work. I'll do anything."

Across the table, Jackie doled out portions of green salad to everyone but Sammy who pulled a face at the sight of the salad bowl.

"You getting a job now will help Matt, but it won't solve everything. I'll contribute when I can as will your dad, but it would be easier if you went to uni in London. There'd be no accommodation costs and you could do your share of looking after Sammy."

"The thing is, the best courses aren't in London. With all the money it's going to cost, the debt I'll have, I don't want to go somewhere substandard."

Sketch's attention drifted back to flicking backward and forward between numerous social media platforms and accident reports. None of the apps she searched or pages she browsed showed any mention of Harry since earlier that afternoon. Nor were there any new messages or texts from her missing crush.

"I'm sure there's a good reason why he's not here," Jackie said. Sketch appreciated the reassurance but though the words went some way to calming her, her stomach refused to stop churning, and her mind tossed thoughts around not caring how rational they were.

Sometimes, aside from the physical sensations afforded by her body, being human didn't feel that different to being back in the Core and messing things up.

"But why isn't he replying to my messages? Have I done something wrong? I don't think I have."

There came a resounding chorus of "no's" from around the table.

"It's not your fault, Sketch," said Jackie. Sketch raised her eyebrows. "Something might have prevented him being here but if not then it's his failing. No one in their right mind would stand you up. "

"You're biased," said Sketch. This wasn't the first time she liked a boy and been disappointed when it didn't play out like a movie and her confidence had taken a plummet.

"Biased I might be but that doesn't mean I'm wrong. I'm sorry Sketch but if the boy doesn't have a good excuse he's a fool."

Sketch attempted a smile and was buoyed by having her adopted family around her. They were amazing and so much more important than boys, even if boys could make her buzz and sparkle.

"I suppose. Thanks guys."

From the corner of her eye, Sketch noticed a flashing notification coming from her phone. It showed a new photo post from Mae. The filtered image jumped out at Sketch, causing her to drop her phone and her grasp on breathing. A rush of adrenaline raised the temperature of her body, making it seem to pulsate with the rapid beating of her heart organ.

"Oh!" Tears collated in small pools around her tear ducts and she urged herself not to cry. Not crying and managing to control her breathing at the same time proved impossible: in fact she was failing at both.

"What on earth is it, Sketch?" Asked Jackie, vocalising the concern on Matt and Ashling's faces.

Sketch strained to speak but her efforts resulted in a blather of snot, choked sounds and irrational gasping and panting noises like she was trying to impersonate the noise of someone revving an unresponsive engine. She bent down and retrieved her phone from where it landed on the carpeted floor. She handed it over to Ashling who sat close to her, still unable to tell them what was wrong. The image of Harry with his arms around another girl and his tongue half way down her throat remained imprinted in her retina. Not any girl, but the worst possible blonde-haired teen she could imagine: her romantic nemesis, Britney.

Chapter Fifty

DESPITE JACKIE INSISTING Sketch stay the night at theirs, she was adamant she wanted to return home, to her own bed at Trevor's flat. If she slept at Jackie's house she would not be able to process her emotions. More than ever she wanted to revert to her former life as a computer energy. Being a human sucked. Anytime something good happened it could be wiped from existence in an instant by sadness, anger, betrayal and boys.

"If you really want to go home Matt will walk you there," said Jackie, her face half frown, half concern and kindness. Sketch shook her head. She blew her nose for the umpteenth time, wondering again where all the snot came from. Where she came from nasal fluids didn't exist, noses didn't exist.

"I'm going with you anyway," said Matt. He held out her coat for her so all she had to do was slot her arms its holes.

"Thanks," she muttered through a snuffle. The offending photo post still displayed on her phone.

"Delete it," said Ashling, reaching for the mobile. "Otherwise you'll torture yourself looking at it all the time. "That girl better not come anywhere near me or she'll not know what's hit her." She swiped the screen, entered Sketch's password INCO2000 and removed the photo.

"It's an unfortunate coincidence," Jackie said giving Sketch a goodbye embrace. "But the person to blame here isn't Britney, the fault is with Harry. She might not even be aware the two of you are close."

Ashling emitted a large snort. "Whatever. She's still never going to be on my friends list. Sketch, you message me anytime. Doesn't matter if it's the middle of the night." She gave Sketch a quick embrace as Matt shepherded her up the stairs, towards the front door.

The sun had not yet disappeared from the London skyline as the pair left the house.

"Don't let him get to you," said Matt. "He's not worth it and if he can do something like this then him and Britney deserve each other."

Tears began to roll down Sketch's smooth skinned face, adding to the blotchy effects of too much crying. Why wouldn't Matt shut up? The last thing she wanted was to talk about Harry and Britney. She gulped back a sob.

"Hey there," said Matt. He pulled up in front of her and manoeuvred her to the side of the pavement out of the way of other pedestrians. He wiped away the moisture channelling down her face with his thumb and kissed her forehead. "Please don't cry. You're so lovely and gorgeous and you make me laugh all the time. Somehow you always know what to say."

"Not now, I don't." Sketch's brain skipped back a track, realising what Matt had said. "You, you think I'm gorgeous?" She was scared to look up in case her ears had misheard his words. In such cases, humans made a joke of things. She could make light of it, but as her eyes shifted upwards towards him all she saw was a smile. The smile first seen from the safety of the Core when she never imagined coming face to face with him in the same world. She responded with a small smile of her own.

"Of course, I do. Look at you."

"So are you," said Sketch, then freaked out in her head having said the unsayable. She wished she had long hair like Ashling, or the extensions Mae tried to convince her have attached, so she could hide her expression behind them. This must be the reason people chose to grow their hair long. Instead, hers grew in funny coloured spikes.

Matt's head grew closer to hers, so Sketch could feel his breath on her forehead. She attempted to process the moment, but it wasn't like any of her other human experiences. As they stood head to head time froze, an aura of anticipation flowing with increasing strength between them. If the pair were in the Core their auras would be bright and fizzling with sparks.

Just as Sketch began to wonder how long they would be locked into this intense, private moment, Matt leaned in and gently placed his lips on hers. Her body soared as he kissed her. *Oh, my first kiss. This is what it feels like.* The thought floated through her mind battling for attention with her lips and the sensation of Matt holding her close. She was kissing the boy Matt.

As she savoured this new human thing, Matt pulled away.

"Sorry, Sketch. I shouldn't have done that." The tenderness he displayed seconds before disappeared, replaced by a rigid, formal version of himself.

Sketch blinked hard. She raised her fingers to touch her lips where Matt had kissed her. What had changed?

"No, it was nice," she said. "I liked it."

"But it's not right, is it?" Matt's hands were planted in the pocket of his jeans, his gaze falling upon his shoes.

"Why?" Sketch's joy continued to drain away.

"It's just not. Look, I'm sorry. This is wrong. I didn't mean to. Sorry, I've got to go."

Sketch looked for words as Matt turned and slouched off down the road. The problem was she didn't know what to say. What had happened to change a magical moment into a mixed up mess of indecipherable negative emotions? It was a wonderful, beautiful, life changing moment, but his parting words destroyed it all, stomped all over her dream fulfilment. Every time she thought something amazing was going on with a boy, she ruined it. It must be her fault cos it didn't happen to everyone else. Other people managed to have boyfriends, girlfriends, lovers, husbands and wives. It came down to one thing; she wasn't human and never would be.

Chapter Fifty-One

TREVOR'S HEAD was stuck into research about community libraries after his conversation with @Library_Warrior64 when he heard the sound of Sketch's feet stomping up the stairs, followed by the noise of her key not quite turning in the Yale lock. He shut down his laptop and shuffled the papers underneath a nearby cushion. What he didn't expect was the black cloud which hovered over Sketch's head and the storm of emotions raging on her face as she made it through the door.

"Young 'un, whatever is the matter? You look like someone swapped all the clothes in your wardrobe for M&S elasticated waist trousers and ugly plastic clogs." He opened his arms, inviting her in for a hug but she recoiled, wrapping her arms around herself like a straitjacket. Ignoring her, Trevor gathered her up in his arms prompting the storm within her to let forth a deluge of tears.

Only when she began to attempt to speak did he pull away, unable to make out what she wanted to say with her words smothered by his jumper. Cleaning snot stains off his designer wear was also at the back of his mind.

"Harry kissed Britney, I kissed Matt, I hate boys, I hate Britney."

She gulped down air. "And I hate being human. This isn't my home. I need to go home, I don't belong here, and I want Inco."

As it all spilled out, Trevor struggled to get to grips with what had happened, who had kissed who, why and how on earth Britney was back on the scene.

"Slow down, one thing at a time. What happened with Harry? Last thing I heard you were both having dinner with Jackie and the gang."

She recounted the events of the evening which resulted in her current state, while Trevor handed her tissue after tissue, made what he thought were the right noises and stroked her back at moments when she looked at risk of hyperventilating. He had no paper bags in the flat and was unaccustomed to dealing with distraught females, a major failing in his flatmate skills he thought. It crossed his mind to message Begw who, despite not being much better at such things, was at least female and would be company, things being easier when shared. Then he remembered Begw's betrayal and tutted at himself for falling into old habits. He could handle this, men cried after all. He himself was partial to a good blubber and had even been known to well up at bad Australian soap operas. Not that he would admit it, even if tortured or bribed.

"That Britney's a, well I won't say what, but you know. Just bin off this Harry and move on."

"I don't see why I feel like this. Why is everything mega confusing? How can I be upset, angry and betrayed by Harry and at the same time gutted that Matt ran away after kissing me?"

"Emotions are messy things. It's all part of being human. I'll bet you, you can't find a single person over the age of fourteen who hasn't felt like you do at one time or another."

To Trevor, Sketch looked more human than she ever had. Her banishment to his world proved a success in terms of learning how, but why such a harsh lesson? It squashed her bounce and positivity and he knew it would be that little bit harder for her to get it back this time round.

"Sausage sarnie?" He asked with a hopeful smile.

"No, thanks though. I couldn't eat anything. Think I'll just go to bed."

Trevor patted her on the leg. "If you need me, no matter what time of the night, you wake me up?" Behind his back he crossed his fingers, making a wish for Sketch to sleep soundly - they both needed their beauty sleep. He shoved a bundle of tissues into her hand. This BFF stuff wasn't so hard after all.

"Night." Sketch's voice was close to inaudible and he wanted to shake Harry and Matt.

"Night, young un." He watched as Sketch dragged herself to the bathroom to brush her teeth, going through the mechanics of getting ready for bed. Sitting motionless until he heard her shut the bedroom door and settle down for the night, Trevor pondered his next move.

He pulled out his phone and texted Jackie asking her to pop into the library tomorrow at lunchtime. Together they could work out the best way to give the stranded computer energy the support she needed. That done, he flipped open his laptop with the intention of cracking on with the campaign work but found he didn't have the stomach for it. "You energies have a lot to answer for," he said to the blank screen in front of him. "Sketch deserves a break. Is there nothing you can do to get her back to your world?" He paused for a moment, as if half expecting a response but none came, and with a sigh worthy of an Oscar, he closed the lid and filed his paperwork away. Before going to bed he checked his phone but as yet Jackie hadn't replied. It looked like they would have to wait for tomorrow to tackle this latest teenage crisis.

Chapter Fifty-Two

NOT WANTING him to know her plans, Sketch waited until Trevor's snoring signalled he was asleep. His snoring was a noise she thought could be recorded and used to torture people into confessing their deepest darkest secrets. It consisted of enormous crescendos of nose snorting, breath puffing and moments of silence which Sketch had taken to be death when she first moved in. She had rushed through and shaken him awake the first time she heard the elephant-like sound of his slumber.

She crept out of her room and into the flat's open plan lounge/kitchen. Enabling the torch app on her phone, she knelt down in front of Jackie and Matt's old computer, the one she used to live inside, and held her breath. At an initial glance everything seemed the same. The machine looked like a shell and she wondered if her mind and her eyes were playing tricks on her. Sometimes that happened when people got in a state, and all the stuff about Matt and Harry made her head spin until her brain felt like it needed to be wiped and rebooted or at the very least defragmented. But she could swear when slinking off to her room earlier, ready to coddle herself in a blanket of sadness, that a faint light blinked on and off from the casing of the computer. That meant one thing: hope. Life in the human world had taught her many things, one of which was the resounding capacity people held in their hearts for hope. Even when things were at their bleakest, hope of something better helped them ride through the difficult times. But as much as she loved her friends, the adopted family who huddled their wagons around her, she wanted more than anything else to return to the Core and life in her own world. The tiny blinking light filled her with the hope this was possible. She sat watching the minutes tick by on her phone with her fingers and legs crossed.

"Come on, please, I know you're in there," she pleaded in whispers to the computer. Thirty minutes passed and as she started to come to terms with the idea she had imagined it, something whirred inside the casing of the PC. "OMG, OMG, OMG." She clasped the sides of the casing and felt a slight vibration from the metal. Something was there. "What can I do?"

As if in answer to her question, a tiny green light began to pulse next to the power switch. She stared, trying to decipher its meaning but it didn't make sense to her. *Focus Sketch, focus,* she thought to herself. The Core had to be sending her a message but what was the key? She closed her eyes and clenched her fists in concentration. Ah, that was it, the resource she needed to decode their communications was inside of her. A light switched on inside her head as she combed through the data downloaded to her before she left the Core many months before.

With the answer accessed, she flicked off the torchlight, so she could better see the dots and dashes of Morse code by which the messages were being transmitted to her.

"Sketch, what are you doing sitting here in dark?"

She jumped, her heart pounded, and her stomach churned on hearing Trevor's voice interrupting her concentrated efforts. Harsh artificial light forced her to blink and rub her eyes, as Trevor flicked on the wall-mounted power switch. The computer continued to flash at her.

"It's working." She gestured to the machine. "Look, there's a light and they're talking to me. You know what this means? I can go home."

Trevor scratched his head. "Are you sure? I mean, it's late. You could be dreaming. I could be dreaming come to think of it."

"No, really. It's sending me messages by Morse code." Seeing he still looked bewildered, Sketch grabbed his hand and pulled him down to sit in front of the computer, so he could view things from the same angle as her. Trevor squinted at the lights, mouth open wide.

"You see?" She said. "They're communicating, using a code, Morse code."

"I don't know Morse code. What are they saying? Why has it suddenly started working?"

Sketch looked excitedly that Trevor. "I don't know why it's working now, but what they're telling me are the things I can fix, the parts needed, the modifications required for me to return to the Core. And the thing is there's nothing I need that's not in the flat. I can fix it tonight." Sketch stood up and started to spin around.

"Sketch! What are you doing young un? You're making me dizzy. Come and sit down for a sec, we need to talk about this."

Spinning at speed filled Sketch with adrenaline and a sense of her former life in the Core. She completed one final spin before slowly returning to the carpet next to Trevor. "Sorry, just imagine, imagine being away from home with no chance of returning and suddenly someone gives you a way back. That's how it feels, that's what's happening to me and the spinning, well I'm just so excited." Sketch glowed as Trevor stared at her.

"I can't imagine how you're feeling. It's great. It's amazing. It's an actual miracle. But you can't go in the middle of the night without saying goodbye to anyone."

Sketch shook her head, "I'm not so sure anyone will care. Not after tonight. They won't miss me. I know you will, but I'll still be there inside the computer. All you need to do is to turn it on wait until it boots and then talk to me. I'll be there observing you."

"Will you be able to reply? Will we get to have an actual conversation?" said Trevor.

In the semi-light of the approaching early morning dawn Sketch saw the worry on Trevor's face. She knew lying was wrong but remembered a conversation with Maud, before she died. Maud told her that sometimes a white lie was okay if it saved someone's feelings.

"Yes, of course. It'll be like I am here in the room except I won't have a body, spiky blonde hair or cute clothes." She leaned over and kissed him on the cheek. He turned away, but she knew he was blushing. "So, here's what I'm going to need."

Chapter Fifty-Three

JACKIE WAS BEING CHASED through mountains by ticks on wheels and was close to toppling off the edge of a rugged cliff side when her body shook her awake. She rubbed her eyes noting again that her vision was deteriorating, a sign of her age. The events of the previous night tumbled back into her thoughts and she gave a groan and rolled over to the other side of the mattress to check the time on her old-school bell-topped alarm clock. She blinked again thinking her dodgy eyesight was playing tricks on her, but no amount of eyelash flapping could change the time on the clock face. It was ten past ten in the morning.

"No!" she groaned. Despite it being a Sunday morning, she wanted to get up and do things. Primarily to pop round to see Sketch and take her for breakfast. Perhaps a chat and a full English breakfast would help shift her mood a little. Goodness knows poor Sketch seemed to be falling victim to all the crises of teenage life one after another. The least Jackie could do was to provide some kind of motherly care and concern in absence of any parents. *It could be worse,* she thought, *Sketch could still be crushing over Matt. That would lead to no end of complications and angst.*

Keen to get up and get things moving, a painful throbbing across her temples made Jackie start slowly.

"Matt? Can you bring me up a cup of tea and my mobile?" The benefits of having a teenage son could be counted on one hand but getting a cup of tea in bed was one of them. As she waited, she thought through what she might say to Sketch to make her feel better about the situation with Harry. At least the Britney drama appeared to have stopped her imagining Harry might be Inco, but that in itself led to another impossible to broach subject.

Just as Jackie was in danger of drifting back to sleep a tap came on her door.

"Come in, Hon."

Through the door came Ashling, steaming hot mug of tea in her hand and Jackie's mobile phone tucked under her armpit.

"Oh," said Jackie. "What's happened to Matt?"

Ashling put the cup of tea on the unit next to Jackie's bed, careful not to spill and shrugged. "I don't know. He's been mooching around all morning like a bear with a sore head. Do bears suffer from sore heads?"

Jackie sighed. "Your guess is as good as mine. Thanks for the tea though."

"Oh, and here's your phone. Been buzzing a lot this morning. You're popular."

Jackie sipped at her tea. She savoured the moment the warm soothing liquid trickled down her throat into her stomach as if it had some kind of reviving powers beyond just simple rehydration. She beckoned Ashling to pass her the phone.

"Really? I'm not expecting to hear from anyone. You should have woken me."

"Sorry Jackie. You looked really tired last night, and everyone needs a lie in now and again."

Popping on her new specs, Jackie scrolled quickly through the alerts displayed on the home screen of the phone. A plethora of voicemail, texts, WhatsApp and emails dominated the screen. All of them from Trevor. Primal panic jolted Jackie upright in her bed.

"Right, we need to go now. Get Matt, whatever he is doing, just get him." Jackie gulped down the remainder of her tea scalding both her tongue and throat in the process. Selecting the last missed call from Trevor she called his phone. It rang and rang and rang with no answer. Without bothering to leave a voicemail Jackie redialled. "This isn't good," she said out loud to no one but herself. She grabbed a pair of jeans from the floor where she'd thrown them the night before, a thing she always told the young people not to do. She threw on her clothes, creating an uncoordinated look she didn't have time to care about, before dashing through the house to find Ashling and Matt.

"Jeez mum, what's the panic? Is there a shortage of decaf organic tea bags and we have to stock up?" Matt rolled his eyes.

"Message from Trevor. Millions of messages from Trevor," panted Jackie, slightly out of breath from the dash to get dressed. "Sketch has fixed the computer or is about to fix it. He said something about lights and her planning to go."

"Go where?" asked Matt, now listening intently.

"Doh! Back to the Core of course," said Ashling. "Where else would she go? It's what she's been trying to do since she got stuck here."

Matt screwed his eyes up and ran his hands over his face. "She can't go, she can't."

Jackie examined the expression on her son's face. Perhaps the situation between Matt and Sketch had changed after all.

"She might have gone already, hon. Let's get around there now. I can't get hold of Trevor at the moment, so you keep trying him on the way. I need to phone Clare."

"Who is Clare?" asked Ashling and Matt at once.

"It's a long story. I promise I'll tell you, but the priority is to get to Trevor's now before Sketch does anything rash. I think this thing with Harry's hit harder than I thought."

"You two go on ahead I need to sort out Sammy. I'll follow on," said Ashling. Jackie nodded, pushing Matt towards the front door. "See you soon."

The pair began to run, and Jackie started to regret skipping the gym or deciding not to go jogging all of those times because it was a weekday or because it was a weekend. She gestured Matt to go on ahead while she slowed down enough to phone Clare. Her call was connecting as she caught up with Matt. He was stuck behind a police cordon.

"What?" She asked Matt.

"Feds say it's a security alert. The whole area's sealed off."

Jackie wanted to cry. There was nothing more she could do. Her last hope was that Trevor could talk some sense into Sketch. Or at least stall her long enough for them all to say goodbye.

Chapter Fifty-Four

WHEN CLARE'S phone rang she was in the bath. Gardening took it out of you, as did stressing about your partner being from another world and there was nothing more relaxing than a nice, long soak in soapy water with bubbles created by herbal bath potions. She laid back, picked up a book from the unit on the side of the bath tub, dispensed of the bookmark and sunk into the fictional world of the latest novel borrowed from the library. Lost in the pages of her book, she failed to hear the ringing of the phone from the living room. Not until Michael banged on the door, opened it gently and popped his head into the steamy bathroom did she realise anything was wrong.

"Sorry to bother you love but it won't stop ringing. It's that Jackie, the one you talked to about Sketch. She's rang you five times in a row and left voice messages. I'm guessing it's important, either that or she's your new stalker," he said.

Clare lurched upwards causing soapy bubbles to spill over onto the bathroom floor.

"Give it here," she said. "It's probably nothing. Best check though." Michael handed the phone over as she dried her hands with a nearby bath sheet. She grimaced as she listened to the messages left on her voicemail by Jackie. Giving the phone back to Michael, she stepped out of the bath tub and began the process of drying and getting dressed.

"We've got to get over there," she said. "Sketch, she's made the computer work and is planning to attempt to send herself back to its inside."

"What? She can't go back, we're not there anymore."

"But she doesn't know that," said Clare struggling to get her trousers on. "She thinks now the computer is back and working she'll find you all there, she'll find the world just as she left it."

"Where does she live?"

"Somewhere in Camden. I'm not sure exactly where and the student records are held at the college. Use my phone to text Jackie while I'm getting dressed. Ask her what's going on. Tell her we're on our way and get Sketch's address."

Clare retrieved the rest of the day's clothes from the laundry basket where they had been chucked before her bath, and dressed in a haphazard fashion which left her t-shirt inside out and her socks unmatched. Knowing her curly red hair would be frizzy from the humid air she grabbed a discarded hair tie and bundled her wayward locks into a tangled bun.

"Any luck with Jackie?" she shouted, picking up her bag while running down the stairs.

"Yes, she's stuck. The area's sealed off by the police. You don't think it's to do with Sketch, do you?"

Clare raised her eyebrows. "I doubt they'd be out in force because a teenage girl claims to be an energy from inside a computer. Oh sorry, I didn't mean to sound sarcastic," she said as his face fell. "It's probably a security alert."

"Still, if they can't get there neither can we."

As they met at the bottom of the staircase, Clare rubbed his back and kissed him on the cheek. "No, but we should go over there so we're close by when they open the road up."

She stopped. A tear tumbled down his face from his left eye until it met with the dark stubble growing up from his chin. She reached into her bag for a disposable tissue, gently wiping away the salt water. If only she could take away his pain so easily.

"Hey, you, it's going to be fine. We'll get there before anything happens."

"What if we don't? I should have told her who I was. How can I not have told her?"

"You did what you thought was right. All we can do now is to make it okay for Sketch. Come on." Clare steered him towards the door, snatching the keys for the van from the wooden hand-made key rack hanging on the wall.

Cars, buses, bikes and couriers lined up in the roads in front of them as they attempted to turn right into the main spine road in the direction of Trevor's flat.

"Grrrr," said Michael whose whole body sat rigid on the seat. He looked ready to explode and launch himself out of the top of the van. "Why is it so bad at this time of day?"

"Probably a knock-on effect from the road closure." Clare glanced across to the passenger seat. "Nothing I can do I'm afraid."

The pair sat in an uncomfortable silence, the air charged with tension and the occasional frustrated sigh from Michael between his attempts to check for traffic updates on Clare's mobile.

"How did it come to this? This isn't my world. I'm not supposed to be here and now the only person who could understand me is leaving."

Michael's words stung Clare, her body reacting as if rubbed with stinging nettles. She had been at the centre of his world for so many years that it seemed unfathomable he would consider anyone else as close to him as her. She bit her tongue. Now wasn't the time or the place to interrogate their relationship for flaws.

"Michael, the traffic isn't going to get any better. Get out and run there. It's your best chance of stopping Sketch doing something foolish."

His face brightened. "You sure?" He asked, undoing his seatbelt.

"Yes, just go."

He pecked her on the cheek and dashed from the van, along the pavement overtaking the line of stationary transport.

Chapter Fifty-Five

TREVOR ANSWERED the intercom which allowed access to his flat, opened the door and waited for his visitors including Michael to trudge up the four flights of stairs.

"Where is she?"

"Sorry, it took us so long. Traffic."

"Sketch?"

People piled into the living room, out of puff, sweating and anxious. Trevor let them all in, looked from one to one and shook his head. "I'm sorry, she's gone." He grimaced as Jackie's hand went straight to her mouth and her eyes filled with tears.

"I tried to stop her, but it's what she wanted." He took a sheet of A4 paper from the coffee table. "She left this. Wanted me to give it to you, Jackie." He handed her the paper covered by loopy handwriting in pink pen which seeped through to the other side. Jackie took it from him and began to read.

"Dear Jackie, I think right now you'll be feeling mad at me, perhaps sad because I didn't stop to say goodbye. Please don't think this means I don't care. You have been my family, like the mum I never had. I will never forget how you welcomed me, a strange stranger from a fantastical realm, into your home. And I almost felt like I belonged here in your world, with boys, sausages, friends and adventures, but it's not my home and more than ever, I wish to be myself again.

Last night, going back to the Core became more than a possibility. Something brought the computer back to life and they asked me to return, to return with all the learning I acquired about the human world and all you amazing people who live in it. Most of all I'm looking forward to seeing my dearest of friends, Inco. I think he's the one for me, the energy for me that is.

Some might say I'm being selfish and cowardly in going without saying goodbye. They are right, because I've grown to love you and Matt, Ashling, Sammy, Trevor, Begw and all my friends so much. My human heart would break to say farewell to you all face to face for a second time.

Remember you can talk to me anytime, now the computer is working again. Tell me tales of your lives, your loves and share your human hope. Give everyone my love.

I'll see you from the other side.

Love, hugs and sausages,

Sketch."

A thick silence drenched the room. Jackie fiddled with the sheet of paper, fussing it with her fingers. Nobody spoke, and the emptiness was filled with their thoughts, thoughts so loud they could almost be heard by everyone.

I should have told her I loved her.

I could have stopped her going to back to nothing.

I can't imagine the world without Sketch.

It's like someone has died.

Regardless of the thoughts and wishes of those gathered in the flat, Sketch had gone.

Trevor wondered how long they could stand there in a state of limbo. His thoughts were interrupted by the repeated buzzing of the intercom. He lifted the receiver. "Hello? Oh. Come on up."

"Who is it?" asked Matt.

"Begw and err some women who says she's a friend of Jackie."

"That'll be Clare," said both Michael and Jackie.

Trevor let the two women in, stopping himself scowling at Begw as he ushered them into the living room. Clare looked at Michael with questioning eyes.

"I'm too late, love."

"You mean she's gone back? Right now, she's in there?"

All eyes twisted in the direction of computer.

"Can she hear us?" asked Matt.

SKETCH HOVERED by the observation deck, the area of the Core designated for viewing human users of the computer. Her aura lacked sparkle or light. What swirled around her thoughts were the pulses of the One.

"I am not the One you know. It has gone, recycled because of breakdown. All former energies have been transformed. We welcome you back because you have learned, you have superior information about the human users. You are now qualified and indentured to serve the functions of the Core."

She stared outwards, watching as familiar faces of her friends, family and college tutor appeared in front of her being, and the not so familiar image of Inco, in the human form of Michael.

What have I done? I'm stuck, stuck in this world.

Join my mailing list

If you've enjoyed Stuck in Your World and want to receive emails with news, exclusive content AND a free short story, you can sign up to my mailing list from my website.

Sign up at www.anjcairns.com

I don't send lots of emails and you are free to unsubscribe at any time.

Acknowledgments

Writing your first book and letting it loose in the world is a scary thing. Writing your 2nd book is no less terrifying. But we made it. More and more, I've come to appreciate how it takes a tribe to publish a book. My tribe is full of amazing people who have cheered, designed covers, beta read drafts, edited and proof read. They've given me snippets of information, dried my tears, stuck by me while I struggled with depression and couldn't write and done cartwheels when the book became a readable document (I'm might be lying about the cartwheels).

Thank you to Jennie Rawlings Serifim Design for Publishing for another beautiful cover. Cheers and hugs beta readers/proofreaders/amazing friends Laura Goodwin, Hayley Reed, Cerian Lloyd Jones, Melanie Kearney. And a special 'diolch' to Cerian for all the Welshness. To Neil Tester for creating the best peer support Facebook comments feed ever. FACT (I'm very 2014).

A shout out to all my Tottenham cheer team but particularly to my Women In Tottenham friends (and James & Matt) for nights of we'll just have one cocktail fun at Craving Coffee.

In the writing world, a big thanks goes to Nichola. Charalambou of Creative Writes for feeding my creative brain and Adam Forest-Wilsher for being the best wine waiter.

Thanks to my family for being there, regardless.

And last but in no way the least, thank you gorgeous readers for taking letting Sketch and her friends into your world. She loves you all. Stay tuned for further adventures…

Anj

About the Author

Anj Cairns lives in North London, loves all things books, writing, reading and food.

Also by Anj Cairns: Life in Your World - Your World series book 1

  facebook.com/anjcairnsauthor

  twitter.com/anjipowerr

  instagram.com/anjipower

Lightning Source UK Ltd.
Milton Keynes UK
UKHW01f0629090818
326991UK00001B/72/P

9 781999 794415